WESTERN WP PROMISES

SHIPMENT 1

Cowboy Sanctuary by Elle James
Dade by Delores Fossen
Finding a Family by Judy Christenberry
The Family Plan by Cathy McDavid
Daddy's Double Duty by Stella Bagwell
The Sheriff's Son by Barbara White Daille

SHIPMENT 2

A Bride for a Blue-Ribbon Cowboy by Judy Duarte
A Family for the Rugged Rancher by Donna Alward
The Doctor Wore Boots by Debra Webb
A Cowboy's Redemption by Jeannie Watt
Marrying Molly by Christine Rimmer
Frisco Joe's Fiancée by Tina Leonard

SHIPMENT 3

Dancing in the Moonlight by RaeAnne Thayne
One Tough Cowboy by Sara Orwig
The Rancher's Runaway Princess by Donna Alward
A Taste of Paradise by Patricia Thayer
Her Cowboy Daddy by Cathy Gillen Thacker
Cattleman's Honor by Pamela Toth
The Texan's Secret by Linda Warren

SHIPMENT 4

Fannin's Flame by Tina Leonard
Texas Cinderella by Victoria Pade
Maddie Inherits a Cowboy by Jeannie Watt
The Wrangler by Pamela Britton
The Reluctant Wrangler by Roxann Delaney
Rachel's Cowboy by Judy Christenberry

SHIPMENT 5

Rodeo Daddy by Marin Thomas
His Medicine Woman by Stella Bagwell
A Real Live Cowboy by Judy Duarte
Wyatt's Ready-Made Family by Patricia Thayer
The Cowboy Code by Christine Wenger
A Rancher's Pride by Barbara White Daille

SHIPMENT 6

Cowboy Be Mine by Tina Leonard
Big Sky Bride, Be Mine! by Victoria Pade
Hard Case Cowboy by Nina Bruhns
Texas Heir by Linda Warren
Bachelor Cowboy by Roxann Delaney
The Forgotten Cowboy by Kara Lennox
The Prodigal Texan by Lynnette Kent

SHIPMENT 7

The Bull Rider's Secret by Marin Thomas
Lone Star Daddy by Stella Bagwell
The Cowboy and the Princess by Myrna Mackenzie
Dylan's Last Dare by Patricia Thayer
Made for a Texas Marriage by Crystal Green
Cinderella and the Cowboy by Judy Christenberry

SHIPMENT 8

Samantha's Cowboy by Marin Thomas
Cowboy at the Crossroads by Linda Warren
Rancher and Protector by Judy Christenberry
Texas Trouble by Kathleen O'Brien
Vegas Two-Step by Liz Talley
A Cowgirl's Secret by Laura Marie Altom

> WESTERN WP PROMISES <

Cattleman's Honor

USA TODAY Bestselling Author

PAMELA TOTH

❤ HARLEQUIN® WESTERN PROMISES

Recycling programs
for this product may
not exist in your area.

ISBN-13: 978-0-373-00340-2

Cattleman's Honor

Copyright © 2002 by Pamela Toth

Printed in U.S.A.

When she was growing up in Seattle, *USA TODAY* bestselling author **Pamela Toth** planned to be an artist, not a writer. It was only after her mother, a librarian, gave her a stack of Harlequin romance novels that Pam began to dream about a writing career. However, her plans were postponed while she raised two daughters and worked full-time. Then fate stepped in. Through a close friend, Pam found a fledgling local chapter of Romance Writers of America, and for the next twenty years she belonged to a close-knit group of published writers while penning romances for several lines at Harlequin. When Pam isn't traveling with her husband, she loves spending time with her two grown daughters, antiquing, gardening, cross-stitching and reading.

Books by Pamela Toth

Harlequin Special Edition

Thunderstruck
Dark Angel
Old Enough to Know Better
Two Sets of Footprints
A Warming Trend
Walk Away, Joe
The Wedding Knot
Rocky Mountain Rancher
The Paternity Test
The Mail-Order Mix-Up

Buckles & Broncos
Buchanan's Pride
Buchanan's Baby
Buchanan's Return

Silhouette Romance

Kissing Games
The Ladybug Lady

Visit the author profile page at Harlequin.com for more titles.

In loving memory of my mother, Dorothea Coles,
who inspired and encouraged me.

Chapter One

Ignoring her teenage son's glowering expression, Emily Major shut off the engine of her new pickup truck and slid out from behind the wheel. Heart pounding with excitement, she grabbed a bag of groceries and breathed deeply of the clean Colorado air. In front of Emily was a modest ranch house with a wide, inviting porch, the first home she'd ever had a say in choosing.

"Are you going to sit there all day?" she finally demanded through the open window of the truck.

David hadn't wanted to come here from their home in L.A., but he hadn't wanted his mother and father to get a divorce, either.

Even though the breakup hadn't been her choice, Emily suspected that David blamed her for it as well as for moving him to Waterloo.

David didn't honor her with a reply. His arms were folded across his chest and his head was turned away. His bleached hair was hidden by a baseball cap, and the sun glinted on the small gold hoop in his ear.

Emily had no idea how to reach him anymore. The loving little boy who had believed she'd hung the moon had been replaced by a brooding stranger with a partially shaved head and a permanent curl to his lip. Sometimes the pain in his eyes, brown like her own, broke her heart.

It was for David's sake that she'd uprooted the two of them and her business. She would do anything to keep her son safe, but he hated everything she did. Sometimes she wondered whether he hated her, as well.

With a sigh, Emily dug the new brass key from her purse and headed up the path to the house. She'd been here once before, after spotting the classified ad in a real estate magazine. She'd been desperate to get out of L.A., but David had of course refused to come with her to look at the property—just as he'd refused to believe she would consider moving to the American wasteland, as he called any-thing outside southern California.

They had spent last night in town, sharing a motel room equipped with sagging beds, a bathroom faucet that dripped all night into a rust-stained sink and a black-and-white TV with two channels. Now their suitcases and David's motorbike were in the back of the pickup. The truck with the rest of their belongings was supposed to meet them here this morning.

When she'd driven through the center of the sleeping town late last night, David had made rude comments about the false-fronted buildings, the cowboy they'd seen walking down the wooden sidewalk and the community in general. Finally, Emily, exhausted by the long drive and the uncertainty gnawing a hole in her stomach, had lost her temper and snapped at David. He'd barely spoken since, but at least he'd stopped sneering long enough to wolf down a huge country breakfast this morning at the little café on the rustic main street. Beneath all the bravado and attitude, he was still a typical sixteen-year-old with a hollow void for a stomach.

"What are you doing?" he called out as she lugged the bag of groceries up the front porch steps.

Encouraged, Emily plastered a wide smile on her face and turned around. She pushed her sunglasses back up her nose with her free hand. Despite the cool breeze, the spring sunshine was dazzling. After the cacophony of noise in L.A., the silence here was a sound in itself.

"I'm going inside our new home. Why don't you come and look around?" she invited with a sweeping gesture.

To her surprise and delight, he opened the door of the pickup she'd bought for the move and unfolded his gangly body from the cab. If he walked any more slowly, he wouldn't be moving at all, but she hid her irritation beneath a veneer of patience as she waited for him to cross the yard. He'd shot up this year and the girls back home had started to notice him, one more reason he resented the move.

When he finally joined Emily, their gazes were level, even though she was standing three steps above him. "It's *your* new home," he replied, his attractive features distorted by his hostility. "I'm moving back to Brentwood with Dad."

Dismay pricked Emily's balloon of happiness. She reached out to touch his shoulder, but he jerked away. Letting her hand drop to her side, she bit her lip and debated breaking the news that his father didn't want him. Stuart had a new family now, a wife who was much younger than Emily and a baby conceived before his separation from her. True to form, Stuart had allowed David to believe that Emily's vindictiveness was the reason he couldn't live with his father in his sprawling new showplace, that the court had sided with her, and that Stuart's hands were tied.

"We'll talk about it later," Emily said now, silently calling herself a coward for postponing the inevitable as she juggled the groceries and unlocked the solid front door. It opened directly into the living room, which was minuscule by the standards they were both accustomed to, but was perfectly adequate for the two of them. On one wall was a lovely fireplace built by the former owner with rocks he'd hauled from the surrounding land.

Ignoring David's derisive snort, Emily crossed the wood floor and went through an archway to the cozy dining room. Two big windows trimmed with leaded glass faced east, framing a view of rolling pasture that stretched out like a shaggy gold and green carpet as far as she could see. Twenty acres of that pasture were hers.

Emily tore her gaze from the view and continued to the kitchen. The appliances were outdated, though functional, and would eventually have to be replaced, but the oak cupboards, lovingly handcrafted and polished to a satiny gleam, were as appealing as the first time she'd seen them. Setting down the bag of groceries, she stowed the perishables in the refrigerator.

"Where's my room?" David demanded from behind her. "Or do we have to share, like last night?"

The town's one motel had been booked nearly full with attendees of some local livestock auction, an event that hadn't escaped David's contempt, and they'd been fortunate to get a room at all.

Emily ignored his sarcasm, but his attitude was eating at her patience and spoiling her pride of ownership. "You have your own room," she replied with forced cheerfulness. "You're way too messy for us to be permanent roommates."

Before he could say anything more, she brushed past him, leading the way back through the dining room to a short hallway. As well as three adequate bedrooms, the house had, astonishingly, two bathrooms, one adjoining the master bedroom. She paused in the doorway of the other one.

"This is yours," she said, gesturing, "but

you'll have to keep it picked up, because company will be using it, too." Their home in Brentwood had included a private bathroom off each of its five bedrooms, as well as two powder rooms on the main floor, one bigger than the kitchen in this house.

There was no point in looking back. The past was behind them and the future was hers to determine without asking anyone else's permission.

"Like we'll have any company here," David complained. "We don't *know* a soul in the whole damn state."

"I'll let that one go," Emily replied, hanging tight to her temper, "but any more bad language and your bike stays parked for a week. If you want to ride the bus to school, keep it up."

"Aw, geez!"

"You know the rules," she continued, ignoring his outburst. "I understand how difficult this has been for you, but it's no picnic for me, either."

"The he-eck it isn't," he burst out. "You can work anywhere, but my life and my friends are a thousand miles away!"

"So's the hood who could have killed you!" Emily said without thinking. The boys who'd shot at David while he was jogging before school had never been apprehended. Her son had steadfastly claimed not to have recognized them, nor could he remember anything about their car.

Now his jaw clenched as she touched his arm fleetingly. Flogging him with constant reminders of the incident would get them nowhere. "You'll make friends at your new school," she promised, hoping his appearance wouldn't set him apart from the local kids. "Now let's look at the rest of the house before the truck gets here with our stuff."

For a long moment he returned her pleading stare with an obstinate one of his own. Then he ducked his head, giving her a glimpse of the bewildered child behind the defiant rebel, and stepped aside. Emily pushed open the door to the room directly across from the bathroom.

"This is yours." She let him go in first, knowing how different it was from his former retreat with its custom entertainment center, computer desk and small refrigerator. He stood in the middle of the floor with his shoulders hunched, but at least he looked around. The corner room had windows on two walls. The third held an ample closet and a built-in bed frame with drawers underneath.

David glanced at Emily and shrugged. "It's okay, I guess."

Not surprised, she nodded and quickly showed him the remaining two rooms. Her bedroom would be the one with the adjoining bath that she'd been surprised an old bachelor would bother with, and the other would serve as her office. She planned to turn one of the nearby outbuildings into her studio.

Trained by a respected old master back in L.A., Emily restored rare books. While living in California, she had developed a large client base and she now turned down more commissions than she accepted. Her income, though not on a par with that of her ex-husband, was sufficient to maintain herself and her son comfortably. The only money she accepted from Stuart was the court-ordered child support payments that went directly into David's college fund.

Before she could think of anything else to say about the house, a rumble from outside alerted her to the arrival of the moving truck. Emily was relieved it was on schedule. Once the unloading was done, she and David would have plenty to keep them busy. With the first show of real interest since they'd crossed the California state line, he hurried past her toward the front door.

* * *

"Adam, it's just dinner. Denise Sparks seems like a nice woman. C'mon, give her a chance."

Travis Winchester's voice was as irritating as the whine of a mosquito, and his older brother, Adam, ignored it as he stalked past the feed store cash register to the exit. Adam had enough on his mind without dodging Travis's clumsy matchmaking attempts.

Head down, cheeks burning, Adam pretended not to notice the cashier's smirk or the curious glances from several other customers who had overheard Travis's plea. Adam would have liked to wring his brother's neck. Ever since Travis had married his mail-order bride, he'd been determined to see Adam get hitched, as well.

Dammit, why wouldn't anyone listen when Adam told them he tried never to make the same mistake twice? Except for his daughter, Kim, his marriage had been a huge blunder he had no intention of repeating.

Tugging down the brim of his hat, Adam yanked open the front door of the feed store, bent on escape from Travis's nagging. The bell jangled, and he barely had time to register a pair of startled brown eyes before a woman who'd been pushing the door open from the other direction stumbled forward.

She yelped in surprise as one of her flailing hands knocked his hat off and the other jabbed his ribs. He grabbed her arms, struggling to keep his balance as she fell against him, but their feet got tangled, and they both nearly went down.

"Whoa, steady," he said as she twisted out of his grip. Her hip bumped the front of his jeans, and he sucked in a sharp breath. Before she could do him real harm, he took a prudent step backward.

"Are you okay?" he demanded as her spicy perfume teased his nostrils.

Her topknot had come loose and a thick hank of blonde hair hung down past her ear. "I'm fine," she exclaimed, her cheeks a fiery pink. "Sorry."

Adam had never seen her before, or he would have remembered her. "It wasn't your fault," he assured her, bending down to retrieve his new Resistol before she could step on it. He slapped it against his thigh to knock off the dust and set it back on his head. "Are you sure you're not hurt? We hit pretty hard." He could still feel the imprint of her soft breasts against his chest.

"No, I'm okay." She was medium height,

and she had to tip back her head to look at him. Her brown eyes, beneath feathery brows, were an intriguing contrast to her golden hair, but he realized that she wasn't quite as young as he'd first thought.

She bit her lip, drawing his attention to its fullness, and she tucked the dangling lock of hair behind her ear. He was about to introduce himself when she excused herself abruptly and ducked around him. He turned to follow her back inside and ask her name when he realized he'd forgotten all about Travis, who was watching him with undisguised curiosity. Sneaking one last glance at the blonde's retreating figure in snug tan jeans, Adam went down the front steps with his brother hot on his heels.

"That's a novel way of meeting women," Travis said when they both reached the sidewalk. "Just knock 'em down. If they get back up, ask them out."

"I didn't ask her out," Adam growled as he circled their truck and opened the driver's door. "I don't hit on strange women."

"You don't hit on *any* women," Travis replied. "Strange or otherwise. I've never seen her around before."

"She's probably just passing through town.

Forget about her." That was what Adam planned to do.

A brand-new silvery-blue pickup with fancy wheels and California plates was parked in the space next to his. It looked like something the blonde would drive, since it didn't resemble a ranch rig any more than she did a ranch wife. Her perfume screamed "big city" and the skin where he'd grabbed her arm had been as smooth as warm satin.

Not that he'd noticed.

"Why would anyone who looked like her be passing through Waterloo?" Travis asked as Adam started the truck and backed onto the street. "Is there a movie crew in town?"

Adam shot him a disbelieving glance. "How should I know? Maybe she's here for the auction. In case you missed it while you were gawking, she and I didn't take the time to exchange life stories." He shifted gears and headed down the street, resisting the urge to look around and see if she'd come out of the feed store. Speculating about someone he'd probably never see again was a waste of time he didn't have to spare.

"I wasn't gawking," Travis muttered, "but if I was single, I would have at least gotten her name."

Adam nearly laughed out loud. "Yeah, be-

fore Rory showed up, you were a real ladies'
man." He didn't bother to tone down his sarcasm.

Travis leaned forward to fiddle with the
buttons on the radio. "What am I supposed
to tell Denise about dinner?" he asked over
the sound of fiddle music.

"Tell her whatever you want," Adam replied heartlessly. "I didn't invite her. And tell
that redhead you married to quit trying to fix
me up, or I'll have her shipped back to New
York."

"*You* tell Rory that." Travis leaned back in
his seat and folded his arms across his chest.
"You don't have to live with her."

"Fix your friend up with Charlie," Adam
suggested. "He's single."

"Charlie's been seeing the new nurse from
the clinic," Travis reminded him, looking out
the side window.

Who could keep up with Charlie's social
life? When it came to women, he more than
made up for both his older brothers. "We've
got bigger problems than what to do about
your friend," Adam said bluntly. "While you
were ordering that fencing, I heard that Ed
Johnson sold out."

Travis's head snapped around, and he
gaped at Adam. "Are you serious? Johnson

sold his spread without telling us? Is the deal final?"

Adam nodded grimly as he swung out to pass a loaded stock hauler. "Apparently so."

"Everybody knows how bad we need that land," Travis exclaimed. "Who'd buy it out from under us like that?"

Adam's hands tightened on the wheel. "I don't know, but I intend to make some calls and find out."

Back in the feed store, Emily wandered up and down the rows of work clothes, tack, veterinary supplies and tools, some of which she couldn't begin to identify. Several other customers glanced her way, but she wasn't sure whether their interest was because she was new in town or they'd witnessed her embarrassing collision with tall, dark and rugged.

While Emily was here, she had intended asking the cashier if he knew of anyone who might have puppies for sale, but instead she stopped in front of an elaborately tooled saddle. Pretending to study it, she waited for her cheeks to cool off and her heart rate to return to normal. She could still picture the shock in the cowboy's green eyes right before she crashed into him. He'd been as solid as a tree, and his voice was as rough as the bark on its trunk.

She'd felt like such a clumsy fool, knocking his hat from his head and then nearly stepping on it. He'd grabbed her arms to keep her from falling, and she'd acted as though he was trying to assault her.

She had a vague impression of a strong, weathered face and dark hair, but she'd been too embarrassed to pay much attention. Instead she'd made some inane remark, and then she'd bolted down the first available aisle.

Had she even apologized for almost mowing him down? She couldn't remember. If she was lucky, she'd never have to face that man again.

The only male who should be occupying a place in her thoughts right now was David. This was his first day at the local high school, and Emily remembered how rough that could be. She'd brought him in yesterday to register, but today she'd allowed him to ride his motorbike. Although she hadn't been pleased when Stuart had presented it to him without consulting her, she could understand why David would prefer riding it to being dropped off by his mother or taking the school bus.

She hoped he'd make some new friends, if

the local kids didn't think his hair and clothes were too weird. The boys she'd seen looked pretty conventional, and the woman in the office had certainly seemed startled when she'd first glanced up from her computer and seen David, but she'd been pleasant enough while assisting him with his paperwork.

Now Emily noticed the wall clock above the feed store cash register. The real estate agent who'd sold her the property had promised to send over a contractor to turn the shed into a studio, and the man was coming today. Emily and David had spent all yesterday afternoon emptying an assortment of junk from the small outbuilding and scrubbing down the inside. It already had running water, electricity and a solid floor, but it needed some attention before Emily could set up her equipment and work there in comfort.

She had hoped to visit the local library while she was in Waterloo, but any further exploration would have to wait for another day. She'd buy a newspaper on her way out of town and check the classified ads. Perhaps a dog would ease David's transition. He'd never been allowed a pet before, and now they had room for a menagerie if they wanted. Meanwhile she had a contractor to consult with, an office to set up and dinner to plan.

* * *

"I hate it here." David threw down his fork and slid his chair back so fast that it crashed against the floor. "I want to go live with Dad."

"I know the first day at a new school can be tough—" Emily began.

"They're a bunch of dorks and losers!" David exclaimed. At Emily's pointed glance, he righted his chair. "The building is old and crummy, and it's too small." When he'd gotten home earlier, he'd retreated to his room with the door firmly closed, leaving Emily to put her curiosity on hold until she'd summoned him for dinner.

"Why don't you sit down and finish eating," she suggested now. "Give it a few days—"

"I'm not going back there." His cheeks were flushed and his dark brows were bunched into a frown, but his eyes had a suspicious sheen as he plopped back down. After a moment he stabbed his fork into the spaghetti on his plate.

"What will you do if you don't go to school?" Emily asked, feeling as though she were walking barefoot through a room full of mouse traps. Her own appetite had disappeared with his first angry exclamation. She'd hoped at least one student would make an effort to welcome him.

"I dunno," he mumbled. "Hitchhike back to L.A., I guess. I could find a job at one of the studios. Dad would help me."

Emily clasped her shaking hands together in her lap under the table. "Listen," she said, leaning forward, "I want your promise right now that you won't do any such thing." The idea of him alone on some highway, thumb out, made her stomach turn over.

"You mean get a job?" he asked with a patently innocent expression.

"Don't play dumb! I don't want you hitchhiking under any circumstances." Her voice was sharp, and she had to take a deep breath before she continued. "We've talked about the dangers of accepting rides from strangers."

He rolled his eyes, but at least his frown had faded. "Yeah, yeah, I know." He took a huge bite of garlic bread, his jaw flexing as he chewed. Pretty soon he'd be shaving and Lord knew what else.

"I mean it. I want your promise that you'll talk to me before you do anything like that," Emily repeated.

She waited impatiently for his answer while he swallowed. When he took a drink of milk, she nearly screamed with frustration. "David," she warned.

Finally he bobbed his head. "Okay, I promise."

Emily released the breath she'd been holding. "What about your classes? Your teachers? Anyone good? Anything interesting?"

He shrugged, twirling spaghetti around his fork. "Geometry's all right, I guess, and the Spanish teacher's a babe." He gestured with his hands. "Really built, you know?"

Emily realized he was fishing for a reaction. "But can she teach?"

He looked at her from the corner of his eye, and his mouth relaxed ever so slightly. "Who cares?"

"You're right," she teased. "If you don't learn anything, you can always take the class over in summer school."

He slid down in his chair, and she wondered, as she always did, how he could sit on his tailbone like that and be comfortable.

"Are you behind in your classes?" she asked.

"Are you kidding? I'm way ahead in most of them. There are only a couple hundred kids in the whole school, and that's for six grades," he replied. "It's weird having the younger kids right there."

"And did you meet anyone interesting, other than your Spanish teacher?" she persisted.

Instantly his frown was back. "Talk about a bunch of hicks," he grumbled. "You'd think the whole world was into rodeos and cattle ranching. They all dress like Roy Rogers, and they stare at me as though I just beamed down from another planet."

"I'm sure that to the kids around here California *is* a different planet," Emily agreed, "but I'll bet some of them are curious about you. Maybe they're shy. Keep smiling and give them a few days to get used to you."

"You always think everyone is shy, but the truth is that no one likes me here." David shoved back his chair, but this time it didn't tip over. "Is there more spaghetti?"

Emily nodded toward the pan on the stove. "Help yourself. Didn't anyone talk to you?"

"Just one girl," he said as he piled more pasta on his plate and ladled sauce over it. "She showed me where the library was. It only has five computers."

"What's her name?" Emily asked, shaking her head when he pointed first to her plate and then to the stove.

"Her name's Kim. She's in two of my

classes, and I saw her getting on the bus after school."

Emily knew better than to express too much curiosity about the girl. "Do you have homework?" she asked instead.

He stuffed the last bite of garlic bread into his mouth. "Yeah." His voice was muffled, but she ignored the breach in manners that would have sent Stuart into a rage. "I can help you with the dishes first, if you want," David offered.

Emily beamed at him. Sometimes, when she least expected it, the sweet boy she remembered would make an appearance. Stuart had always worked long hours, leaving her to raise their son alone. Until the incident that had gotten David expelled from his old school, she would have said her relationship with him was extremely close. He was still the most important person in her life, but since the divorce, he had built up a wall she couldn't scale.

"School will get easier," she promised rashly. "Give it a little time."

"Can I call Dad?" he asked as he carried his dishes to the counter.

"Sure, after you're done with your homework. Just don't talk too long." She hoped, for David's sake, that Stuart would be home this time, since returning David's calls didn't seem to be a priority.

While David stacked their dishes, she began running water into the sink, followed by a squirt of liquid soap.

"When are we getting a dishwasher?" he asked as he put the leftover salad in the refrigerator.

"After I get the bill for remodeling the studio," she replied. She'd spent a big chunk of her settlement for this place, and she was cautious by nature. "Until then, we do it the old-fashioned way."

Wrinkling his nose at the sinkful of bubbles, he grabbed a towel. "I'll dry."

Two days later Emily was in her office going through the mail when she heard someone knocking. Figuring the contractor must be back from town, where he'd gone to buy more supplies, she hurried through the living room and opened the door without bothering to look out the window.

Standing on her porch was a tall man wearing a black cowboy hat. Speechless with surprise, Emily stared over the top of the reading glasses perched on her nose. His familiar green eyes widened and then his serious expression relaxed slightly. How could the same lines that detracted from a woman's beauty look so fantastic on a man?

"Ms. Major," he said, touching the brim of his hat with his fingers, "we meet again. I'm Adam Winchester. We more or less ran into each other at the feed store the other day."

How had he found out her name and tracked her down so quickly? And *why* had he bothered?

As he waited with an expectant expression, Emily pulled the door partially shut and blocked it with her foot, suddenly aware of her isolation from the main road as well as her neighbors. This wasn't L.A., and the man was probably harmless, but he had gone to the trouble of seeking her out, and she wasn't taking any chances.

"What do you want?" she asked without returning his smile.

His jaw hardened in response to her lack of welcome, and his gaze narrowed, drawing attention to his thick, dark lashes and emphasizing the creases fanning out from his eyes. "There's something important you and I need to discuss," he said forcefully.

Some women would undoubtedly find his interest complimentary, his determination flattering, but Emily was merely annoyed by his persistence. In California she'd been surrounded by truly beautiful women, and she'd been married, so men hadn't been standing in line to flirt with her. Perhaps here in rural Colorado any reasonably attractive woman was fair game, but the last thing Emily had time for was an admirer, especially one who might prove to be obstinate. The best thing for both of them would be for her to make it clear this man was wasting his time.

"I'm sorry you've come all this way for nothing," she said with a dismissive curving of her lips as she shifted the door shut a couple more inches. "It's nothing personal, believe me." As her gaze left his to inadvertently sweep over his long, lean body, she felt a tiny shiver of regret. If she'd been in the market... Her visitor was a walking, talking cowboy fantasy, the total opposite of her sophisticated, successful ex-husband.

"I'm sure you're a very nice man," she continued briskly, before he could respond, "and you're certainly attractive, but I've just moved in. and I really don't have the time or the interest in getting to know you better. If you'll excuse me—"

Before she could close the door the rest of the way, his hand, clad in a worn leather work glove, shot out and held it open. "I hate to burst your bubble, Ms. Major," he drawled, amusement evident in his eyes, "but I'm not here on a social call." His gaze touched her body in a way that left her feeling as though she'd been thoroughly frisked. His smile was back, but it was mocking. "You're an attractive woman, and I hope you won't take this personally," he continued, parroting her words outrageously, "but my visit is strictly business. I'm here to buy your land."

Chapter Two

Adam watched the woman's cheeks turn pink as she absorbed his last statement, and he wondered whether he should have pandered to her assumption that he'd taken a personal interest in her. She was certainly pretty, even with those silly wire-rimmed glasses perched on her pert little nose and a streak of dust down one cheek, but he would prefer a woman who wasn't quite so confident of her own appeal as to assume he'd followed her home like some lovesick pup.

"You're here to buy my land?" she finally echoed, her death grip on the door relaxing enough for him to gently pry it back open.

A frown marred her forehead. "But it's not for sale."

He'd come prepared to negotiate, and he refused to be distracted by the way her full lips shaped each word she spoke. "Everything's for sale if the price is right," he replied. "I'll give you ten percent over what you paid Ed Johnson. Why don't you let me come in, and we'll finalize the deal right now." He wasn't sure what her connection was to the previous owner, but the only possible reason for her to buy the twenty-acre parcel, surrounded on three sides by Winchester land, was to turn a quick profit. Why else would she be here?

He'd actually taken a step forward before he realized she wasn't exactly welcoming him into her home. Nor did she appear the least bit impressed by his offer.

"I might be able to go a little higher," he admitted grudgingly, "but keep in mind that I'm probably the only interested buyer you've got, and my generosity only goes so far."

"Why are you so determined to buy my piddling twenty acres?" she asked. "From what I've seen, there's enough open land in this state to go around."

Adam thought fast while he returned her stare. The reason for his interest was no secret. Why was she pretending ignorance? To throw him off guard?

"My brothers and I own The Running W," he explained, fairly sure he was only repeating what she must already know. "Your land nearly cuts our spread in two, and it's got water we need for our cattle." His senses recognized her perfume from their last encounter, but the distraction was more irritating than enticing. "Let's not dance around the campfire," he added without bothering to conceal his impatience. "Name your price. I've got things to do."

Removing her glasses and folding them carefully, she drew herself up to her full five and a half feet. The curls on top of her head quivered as she thrust out her chin. In its center was a shallow dent that looked as though it had been put there by a sculptor's touch.

"What part of no didn't you get?" she demanded. "My place is not for sale."

Adam sighed. He didn't have time for this. "Call me Adam," he suggested. "And I didn't catch your first name."

"I didn't throw it."

Releasing his hold on the door, he folded his arms over his chest, lifted his brows and waited, a maneuver that worked as well with his fifteen-year-old daughter as it did with his ranch hands.

It didn't work now. "Good day, Mr.—"

"Winchester!" he reminded her right before the door was shut firmly in his face. "Adam Winchester." It took him a full ten seconds to realize he was staring at the painted panel like a fool. Once he'd recovered, he spun on his boot heel with a muttered oath and stomped back down the steps, irritated but undaunted.

Ultimately he'd get what he wanted. When it came to the ranch he usually did. He rarely misjudged an opponent. The little blonde with the big brown eyes might have distracted him temporarily, but she was no match for Winchester determination.

Halfway to his truck, Adam glanced over his shoulder in time to see the front curtain drop back into place. "I'll be back," he muttered as he settled his Resistol more firmly on his head. "We're not done yet."

Plastered against the wall next to the window where she'd ducked to avoid being caught gaping, Emily pressed a hand to her mouth to suppress a groan of embarrassment. What on God's green earth had possessed her to jump to the narcissistic conclusion that Adam Winchester had tracked her down because he'd been dazzled by her feminine charms—and why had she humiliated herself further by telling him?

What must he be thinking? Thanks to her impetuousness, he'd have an amusing story to tell his cronies around the campfire, or wherever cowboys hung out these days. Perhaps it was the rustic saloon she and David had driven by on their arrival. The only thing that could have increased her embarrassment even more would have been for Winchester to catch her watching his departure with her nose pressed to the window.

Good thing that when it came to men with sexy eyes, a killer smile and great buns, Emily was immune—totally, terminally uninterested, especially when the man was also insufferably arrogant, assuming he could waltz in here and demand that she hand over to him this place she already loved.

If her little section of Colorado was so crucial to her neighbor's operation, why hadn't Mr. Johnson sold it to him instead of going to all the trouble of advertising out of state? When she'd bought the land, she'd had no idea anyone else would be interested, but it was obvious now that Adam Winchester would have paid more than she had.

Before accepting Emily's offer, Mr. Johnson had insisted that she make him an unusual promise. He hadn't given her an explanation for his request, and she'd been reluctant to pry, but after Adam Winchester's visit today she was certainly curious. She doubted the promise was legally binding, but that didn't matter. When she gave her word, she tried her best to keep it.

The whine of David's motorbike cut through her thoughts like a chainsaw through butter. She opened the door as he pulled up beside the porch in a cloud of dust and killed the engine.

"How was school?" she asked when he'd removed his helmet.

David swung one long leg over the bike. He came up the steps without meeting her gaze, the helmet tucked under his arm. "It was okay," he said in a flat voice as he brushed past her.

One of the reasons she'd agreed to let him ride his bike instead of catching the bus was that she'd hoped he'd get involved in some after-school activities. Unfortunately, nothing about the new school seemed to interest him so far, not the kids, his new classes or anything else.

"Do you want a snack?" she asked as she trailed after him into the house. Over the last few days, she'd managed to unpack most of their belongings and make the living room presentable, but she had no idea whether her son had even noticed her efforts.

"No, thanks. I'm not hungry," he muttered. Before she could say anything else, he'd gone into his room and shut the door.

A teenage boy with no appetite? Something was seriously wrong. Emily sank onto the leather couch she'd brought from L.A. and stared at the opposite wall, which was blank. The house in Brentwood had been decorated by a big name interior designer Stuart had hired, but Emily planned to fix this one up herself. She'd hoped to enlist David's help, but unless his attitude changed drastically, she couldn't imagine him taking the slightest interest in picking out pictures and bric-a-brac.

She hadn't done anything more about getting a dog, but she wanted to find one before she bought any livestock. She'd need a cat, too, once the remodeling in her workshop was completed. The contractor had promised to send a man out to repair the corral fencing next week. Fortunately, the small stable was sound. It would make a perfect home for the horses she planned to buy.

Emily hadn't always been a city slicker. Growing up near Sacramento, she'd spent as much time as possible on horseback. Over the years she'd continued to ride on occasion. Stuart had never shared her interest—had even seemed to resent it—but she'd taught David to ride. His enthusiasm had waned in the past couple of years, but she hoped having horses of their own would revitalize it. He had to do something besides e-mailing his friends back home.

Meanwhile she removed the chicken from the refrigerator in order to fix his favorite dinner. It was nearly ready when he finally emerged from his room.

"Sweetie, would you set the table?" she asked as she mashed the potatoes.

Silently he complied, while Emily mounded the fluffy spuds into a bowl and fished around for something to talk about.

"Who was that guy I saw leaving right before I got home?" he asked, sparing her the trouble. "The one in the big black truck."

As if they had so many visitors that he needed to be specific. "That was our neighbor, Adam Winchester," she replied as she dished up some peas. "He made me an offer for this place." As soon as the words were out, she wished she could recall them.

David froze in the middle of setting out flatware. "What did you tell him?" His hopeful tone made Emily wince.

She sighed. "We're not selling."

"Why not?" David demanded, his voice rising. "If you got your money back, we could go home where we belong."

"We just got here," Emily told him. "Won't you please give Colorado a chance? Neither one of us belongs in L.A. any longer."

He glowered at her, his knuckles white as he gripped the back of the chair. "I hate it here. The kids are all hayseeds, and they stare at me like I came from Pluto."

Emily ached to see him so miserable. "What about that girl you met?" she asked. "Have you talked to her again?" She still hoped a few of the other students would be friendly enough or curious enough to make the first move.

He jammed his hands into the pockets of his baggy jeans, his shoulders hunching over. "She's busy with her own friends."

"What about the boys?" Emily persisted. "This is a small town, and it's not every day someone comes here from another state. They must have noticed you."

"Like I care," he said with a defensive sneer. "I have plenty of friends."

And a few enemies, too, Emily thought grimly, but she didn't voice her thoughts. "Let's eat before the food gets cold," she suggested as she set the plate of chicken and the bowl of mashed potatoes on the table.

David poured milk for both of them. "Why can't we just go home?" he whined, after they'd helped themselves and started eating.

Emily gave him a long look. "You know why."

His cheeks turned red, and his mouth took on a sulky droop. "Aw, Mom. You just over-reacted," he said. "Nothing really happened."

She set down her fork and lifted her chin. "We've been over this before. We're here now, and we're staying, so you might as well make the best of it."

For a moment he glared back at her defi-antly. Then he shifted his gaze, picking up a drumstick and biting into it without replying.

It was time for a change of subject. "I've been thinking about getting a dog," Emily announced. "We've certainly got the room. Would you be interested in helping me pick one out?"

David had always wanted a pet, but Stuart hadn't liked the idea of an animal shedding on the expensive furniture and carpets of the showplace in Brentwood. Now she watched the emotions play across her son's face. Fi-nally, after an obvious struggle, his brood-ing expression lightened, reminding Emily of his habitual sunny disposition until her divorce from his father. How much David had changed in a little more than a year.

"Can we look for a dog after supper?" He was actually smiling.

Emily had to grin at his enthusiasm. "I need to call on a couple of ads from the newspaper first," she replied. "And don't you have homework?"

David shoveled a forkful of mashed potatoes into his mouth. "Yeah, but only a little," he mumbled. "I did most of it at lunch." He swallowed and immediately took another bite. "I'll do the dishes while you call."

Chores had been one more thing she and Stuart had never agreed on, but she'd been adamant that David learn responsibility. Now that she no longer had hired help in the kitchen, she was doubly glad she'd stuck to her guns despite Stuart's sneering remarks about women's work. Had her husband changed so much over the years, or had she failed in the beginning to see what he was really like?

She hoped the people with dogs for sale were home. "Just for tonight I'll do the dishes while you finish your studying." She gave David a warm smile. Whenever she caught a glimpse of the sweet little boy she remembered beneath the cool adolescent veneer, her determination to keep her son safe at all costs was strengthened. She would have moved to the ends of the earth to protect him. Compared to that, the wilds of Colorado seemed pretty tame.

"Daddy, don't you like the enchilada casserole?" Kim Winchester asked. "Betty and I fixed it special for you because last time you said it was so good."

Adam blinked and glanced down at his plate, surprised to see that he'd only been picking at his food. "Uh, the casserole is great, honey. I've just got a lot on my mind." He gave his daughter a reassuring smile, relieved to see her worried frown melt away.

Since Kim's mother had left when Kim was little, Adam's daughter was the most important person in his life. Call him overprotective, but he remembered how fiercely she'd missed Christie in the beginning. He was determined to make sure no one ever hurt Kim that badly ever again.

To convince her now that he really liked the casserole, and because he'd just realized he was genuinely hungry, he dug into the mixture of meat, corn and tortillas. She watched while he rolled his eyes and chewed enthusiastically. "It's wonderful," he pronounced, mouth full.

Apparently satisfied, Kim turned her attention back to her own meager portion. She was built like her mother, small and slim, and she ate like a bird.

As Adam made an effort to clean his plate before the housekeeper could scold him, his thoughts went back to his earlier visit to his neighbor, Emily Major.

Even though she hadn't bothered to introduce herself, he'd already gotten her name from county records. When he'd first recognized her, he'd felt a momentary twinge of disappointment. He'd been right—she was new to the area. Too bad she would probably be leaving again as soon as he'd bought her out. Under different circumstances he might have enjoyed getting to know her better.

His determination to acquire her twenty acres hadn't changed since she'd turned down his offer, but the negotiations looked to be a whole lot more entertaining than he'd first figured. Now that he'd had time to think about it, he couldn't say he was all that disappointed she hadn't given in on his first try. At least he had an excuse to tangle with Ms. Major again.

"You look like you just beat Uncle Travis at poker," Kim said. "What's going on?"

Her perception startled him. If she was able to read him this easily at fifteen, the next few years could be a challenge.

"I was just thinking about a little land deal I'm working on," he replied, sipping his water.

"Isn't the Running W big enough for you yet?" she teased. "It's already way bigger than any of my friends' ranches."

"You know how we always have to move the cattle out of the eastern pasture every summer," he reminded her. "It's water we need more than land."

When it came to the actual working of the ranch, Kim hadn't yet taken much of an interest. Someday the Running W, begun on a much smaller scale by her grandfather, would be passed on to the next generation of Winchesters. Kim was the only child Adam figured on having. Someday she'd own a third of it. Since Adam had taken over, he'd expanded the operation and put it on a solid financial footing. Too bad the old man hadn't lived long enough to see what a good job his oldest son was doing.

"There's a dance at school in a couple of weeks," Kim said. "Sarah wanted to know if I was going."

At least it wasn't some boy doing the asking. Not yet, anyway. Dances at the high school were well chaperoned. Kim had been allowed to go to several already this year, even though Adam would have liked to keep her locked in her room until she was thirty.

"Is this the reason for the enchilada casserole?" He couldn't resist teasing. "Soften the old man up first?"

Kim looked mildly indignant, but the flush on her cheeks gave her away. "Of course not. All of my friends will be there, and I didn't think it would be a problem."

"Well, if Sarah's parents can drive one way, I'm sure somebody here can manage to pick you up," Adam conceded.

"Billie Campbell got his driver's license." Kim picked up her roll and began tearing it into pieces. "Sarah said he might be able to borrow his dad's car."

Before Kim had finished talking, Adam was already shaking his head. "Billie Campbell lives clear on the other side of town, and I don't want you riding with someone who just got his license."

"Da-ad!" she wailed, dropping the roll onto her plate. "That's not fair. I'm too old for my father to drive me."

"You're fifteen. Life isn't always fair," he

replied evenly, unwilling to argue with her, "but I'll be happy to provide transportation. Let me know what you decide." Billie Campbell was barely sixteen, a mass of hormones with all the sense of a bull calf. Adam might not be able to bar boys like him from the dance or keep them away from Kim, but he wasn't about to let his daughter in a car with one of them behind the wheel.

For a moment she glared at him, lower lip poked out, but then she sighed dramatically. "Okay. Can I at least get something new to wear?"

He chuckled, suspecting he'd just been maneuvered by an expert. "I suppose. If Betty doesn't have time to take you shopping before the dance, let me know, and I'll see what I can do."

"Thanks, Daddy." Kim's smile brought a shaft of relief that, so far, their relationship hadn't been marred by the kinds of arguments some of the other parents were already having with their kids.

"What else is going on with you?" he asked idly as he cleaned his plate.

"There's a new boy at school." She tucked a strand of long, dark hair behind one ear. Six months ago he'd told her she couldn't have them pierced until she turned sixteen.

That had cost him a new parka, he recalled. "I think he's from California," she added. "He's way cool."

Adam blinked. "Who?"

Kim rolled her eyes. "The new boy. The one I was just telling you about."

New boy? Adam's paternal instincts went on red alert. "Have you met him?"

"Not really, but he's in a couple of my classes. He acts so much more mature than the other boys." Kim had friends of both genders, and Adam suspected she got periodic crushes he didn't know about or care to. Someone different might seem pretty slick to a young girl like her. Adam wanted to warn her to be careful, but he didn't know what to say without scaring her or making her clam up.

California! Perhaps the fancy truck Adam had seen in town belonged to the new kid. He was probably Emily's son. If so, he wouldn't be around long enough for Adam to be concerned.

Suddenly, he realized that Betty, his longtime housekeeper, was standing by his elbow waiting to take his plate.

"Are you finished, Mr. Winchester?" she asked. She'd worked for him since right after Christie had left, managing the household, helping to raise Kim and offering a running commentary on Adam's social life, but she had steadfastly refused to call him by his first name. That, she felt, would breed too much familiarity.

On more than one occasion he'd wished she would call him any damn thing she wanted just as long as she kept her nose out of his personal life.

Now he leaned back in his chair so she could clear away his dishes. "Thank you, Betty. As usual, dinner was delicious."

"Thank your daughter," she replied, glancing across the table with a warm smile. "While she was fixing the casserole, I had time to make peach cobbler for dessert."

Adam sat up straighter. Peach was one of his favorites. "The two of you are going to spoil me," he drawled, patting his flat stomach. He was on the move far too much for his weight to ever be a problem.

"You don't have anybody else in your life to pamper you and no prospects on the horizon that I can see, so I guess the job falls to Kim and me," Betty replied with a sniff as she left the room.

Adam had learned from long experience that ignoring Betty's more pointed remarks was his simplest option.

"You don't need anyone else," Kim exclaimed. "Like you've always told me, you and I are a team, right?" Although Christie still lived in Denver, she hadn't played a big part in Kim's life. Christie worked in a gallery there, and a daughter who needed her wasn't a priority. She hadn't remarried, but Adam had long suspected Christie had something going with the gallery owner, who was much older and very successful.

"In a few years you'll meet someone special, and then your attitude will change," Adam told Kim, putting on a woeful expression and shaking his head sadly. "You'll forget your old man even exists."

"Never!" she declared, jumping up to come around the table and throw her arms around his neck. "And I'd never marry anyone who wasn't willing to run the ranch and take care of you in your old age, either."

A sudden image of himself in a rocking chair with gray hair and a blanket over his knees made Adam wince as he returned her hug. "Thanks, sweetie, I can't tell you how relieved I am to hear that," he said dryly. For some reason, he pictured the way Emily Major had looked that afternoon, her cool smile a challenge he found hard to dismiss.

Although remarriage wasn't in the cards, he was still glad that he wasn't ready for that rocking chair just yet.

Emily surveyed her new studio with a sigh of satisfaction. There were several long benches, two with recessed shelves underneath them for her cases of brass hand tools and other supplies. In a corner was a cabinet with drawers for type and a small iron nipping press bolted to the top. On one table were several other kinds of presses and cutters, an electric tooling stove and a grinder for her knives. A file cabinet held correspondence and records of books she had already restored. A fire-resistant safe contained two new projects, a very old family Bible and a sixteenth-century medical handbook. Mounted on one wall was a CD player and speakers. On another was a rack to hold rolls of raw Asahi silk from Japan.

Emily was eager to return to work, but right now she wanted to take a walk along the property line with Monty, the collie she and David had brought home the afternoon before, and see how the fence repair work was going. There was a stiff spring breeze, and the sun was shining. She wasn't ready to shut herself inside with relics from the past, no matter how fascinating.

Monty thrust his cold, wet nose into Emily's hand as if to remind her of his presence. He might not have been the dog they'd set out to acquire, but they'd made an impulsive—and fortunate—detour at the local veterinarian's office on their way to check out a litter of blue heeler puppies at a house on the other side of Waterloo.

Monty's owner had gone into a nursing home, and the vet told Emily he'd nearly given up finding a new family for the middle-aged collie. Lucky for Emily that David had fallen for the dog as quickly as she had. The moment they followed Doc Harmon into the back room of his office and saw Monty curled up on a braided rug by the heater, the dog had stolen her heart. When she was little, she'd always wanted a collie just like Lassie, and now she had one.

"Yes, you're a good boy," she cooed as she stroked his long, thin head. At first he'd been nervous, sniffing everything in the house and startling at the slightest noise. Eventually he'd settled onto his rug by David's bed and slept there through the night. This morning after David had gone to school, Monty stuck by Emily's side like a magnet on a refrigerator door. He minded well. So far she'd had no need to use the leash that matched his red leather collar.

A puppy would have been banned from her studio to avoid any risk of damage to her irreplaceable inventory or expensive supplies, but Monty, well past the chewing and piddling stages, would be great company while she worked.

Emily was about to shut the studio door behind her when the collie's tulip-shaped ears pricked to attention and a low growl rolled up from his throat. Seconds later Emily saw a dust cloud and then she recognized the black pickup coming down her road.

"It's okay," she reassured the collie, glad for his presence. Coming from L.A., she wasn't yet completely at ease with the wide-open spaces surrounding her or the sense of utter remoteness she felt when David wasn't home.

The dog gave her a quick glance and then resumed his watchful stance as the pickup rolled to a stop. Adam Winchester emerged, one long leg at a time and, to Emily's surprise, Monty's feathery tail began to wag in great sweeping strokes.

"Some watchdog you are," she scolded

softly as the dog deserted her for her visitor, who immediately stopped and extended his hand.

From his black cowboy hat to his scuffed leather boots, Winchester was once again dressed like a working cowboy. All he needed was a six-gun strapped to his hip and he could have walked right onto the set of an old Western movie.

"Hello again," he called out to Emily as he patted Monty's head. The dog wiggled like a puppy. "What's Mae Sweeney's collie doing here?"

Monty glanced up at Emily, who hadn't bothered to return her neighbor's greeting. What part of *I'm not selling* hadn't Adam Winchester understood?

"I didn't steal him, if that's what you're thinking," she replied defensively, ignoring her sudden attack of jealousy over her new pet's defection. "I got Monty from the vet. He needed a home, and Doc Harmon said he's got too many dogs already."

"What are you going to do about him when you leave?" Winchester asked as he removed his hat and ran his fingers through his black hair.

"Doc Harmon?" She barely knew the man.

"No, the dog. I'll take him, if you want. We can always make room for one more at the ranch."

First her land and now her dog? What was it with this man? Next he'd be angling after her firstborn. Emily lifted her chin and braced her hands on her hips. "Who said anything about leaving?" she asked in her chilliest voice. "I happen to like it here."

Winchester glanced around them with a speculative expression. "You planning on ranching your twenty acres?" His tone indicated that her property was too small for anything bigger than a pea patch.

"I may," she retorted. "Not that it's any of your business." She'd actually considered buying some sheep, but she no longer had to explain her every action to some man. Let Mr. Hotshot Cattle Rancher think what he liked.

He made a sweeping gesture with his hand. "My property surrounds you on three sides. Everything that goes on around here is my business."

What arrogance! Emily forced herself to saunter over to where he stood with her dog. She would have liked to call Monty back to her side, but it would be too embarrassing if the collie chose to ignore her.

She wished Winchester didn't tower over her by a head, but she refused to let his greater height and the width of his shoulders intimidate her. She was through knuckling under to anyone, and she'd go toe-to-toe or nose-to-nose to hang on to what was hers. This man might make her nervous, but he'd never know it.

"I think you'd better leave." She snapped her fingers at Monty, who ducked his head and slunk to her side.

"Not before you name your price," her neighbor insisted with a gleam in his eye, as though they were sharing a joke.

"A million dollars!" Emily said rashly.

His amusement faded like a light winking out. "You're kidding, right?"

"No," she said. "I'm not. Take it or leave it."

"I'll leave it. Let me know when you've come to your senses." Letting his gaze sweep over her one last time, he jammed his hat back on his head and spun on his heel.

Emily watched him climb into his truck, ignoring the way his jeans molded themselves to his masculine contours. "Don't hold your breath," she called out childishly, arms folded.

He looked down at her from the open window. "You'll sell."

His confident tone sent a shiver of foreboding down Emily's spine. How far was this man willing to go to get what he wanted?

Chapter Three

"How's the land grab going?" Charlie Winchester asked Adam as Travis turned a snort of laughter into a cough that he buried in his fist.

Usually the three brothers worked different parts of the sprawling ranch, each leading his own group of men, but a small bunch of cattle needed moving closer in, so Adam had recruited the other two and a couple of the dogs to ride out with him this morning. Preparation for spring roundup had kept them all too busy for more than the most perfunctory conversation during the past couple of weeks, and this was the kind of day that made a man thankful to work outdoors. The sky above was as blue as Arizona turquoise, and the swaying grasses were dotted with early wildflowers.

Adam's saddle creaked as he turned to look at Charlie. "We're buying the Johnson place, not stealing it," Adam said mildly, refusing to let his youngest brother's comment spoil his mood. "The current owner wants to dicker a little before she lets go, but we'll have what we need in the end."

He still didn't know why Emily Major had bought Johnson's place, but he wasn't about to let that stop him. He realized uneasily that he was actually looking forward to their next sparring match. She was attractive, and his blood was still red, even if he didn't have what it took to hang on to a woman he cared about. He had no intention of getting involved.

"So the rumors are all true," Charlie said. "Johnson sold out to a woman from the left coast. What I don't understand is why he didn't talk to us first. He must have known we'd top anyone else's offer."

"He was a reclusive old man," Adam replied as he spotted a few head of cattle. When they saw the approaching riders, they bunched together, their calves bawling nervously. "Maybe he was getting senile, too. Who knows? It's not important. She'll sell."

"Adam will charm her," Charlie told Travis with a broad wink he didn't bother to conceal from his eldest brother. "By the time he's done with the sweet-talk, she won't know what hit her."

Travis glanced at Adam. "If charm is what's needed, maybe I'd better take over," he said to Charlie behind his gloved hand. "When it comes to dealing with the ladies, our big brother's a little rusty."

"You're a married man," Charlie reminded him. "Rory would hand you your head if you ever looked at anyone else." His dimples flashed as he made a mock bow. "I, on the other hand, am presently unattached."

"What happened to that nurse you were seeing?" Adam demanded. The pretty brunette had been on Charlie's arm so often lately, she might have been stuck there with Velcro. "I thought you two were getting serious."

"Hey, this is Charlie we're talking about." Travis's voice danced with humor. "When have you known him to be serious about anything?"

An expression that could have been hurt crossed Charlie's face, quickly replaced by his usual cocky grin. "She started dropping hints about a ring and a future together," he explained with a shrug. "I figured it was time for a clean break."

"You should think about settling down," Travis told him. "Marriage to the right woman beats single hands-down."

"Yeah, but Rory's already married," Charlie replied with exaggerated petulance, "and you won't share."

"Damn right," Travis agreed. "You had your chance with her."

Five years before, Charlie had decided that Travis needed some help in the romance department, so he located Rory through a pen pal service and persuaded her to come out from New York for a visit. The day of her arrival, Charlie disappeared, leaving Travis to deal with her. By the time Charlie came back, Travis had fallen for her just as his younger brother had planned all along.

Until Charlie managed to convince Travis that he'd never intended her for himself, relations had been strained, to say the least. Ever since then, Charlie had taken full credit for finding his brother a bride, much to Travis's annoyance and Adam's unease. Charlie had been warned he'd spend six months in a line shack with only the herd for company if he even thought about pulling a similar trick on Adam.

Adam signaled the dogs to get the cattle moving while Charlie and Travis fanned out. Adam hadn't yet told Travis that the woman who'd bought the Johnson place was the same one Adam had collided with at the feed store.

"Has this gal got a husband?" Charlie called out. "I could drop by and pay a neighborly visit after church tomorrow, encourage her to sell." Despite his matchmaking talent, Charlie had never tied the knot, and he fancied himself a bit of a ladies' man. Most of the local female population would probably agree. All he had to do was smile and flash his dimples. Women fell like apples from a tree.

Adam wished they were driving a larger herd, so they'd be too far apart for conversation, or that the cattle would bolt, necessitating a wild chase. For once the dogs were doing too good a job keeping them tight.

Adam was tempted to tell Charlie that Emily was married to a pro wrestler from cable television or that she was eighty-five years old and chewed tobacco. "Don't trouble yourself," he said instead, the surge of irritation he felt making him more than a little uneasy. "I'll handle her."

"He's holding out on us," Charlie called out to Travis. "I'll bet you a ten spot she's pretty."

"Adam's idea of pretty is a horse with spots on its butt." Travis glanced pointedly at Adam's Appaloosa.

Adam fiddled with the bandanna he'd tied around his neck. The other two would be on him like dogs on fresh meat if they suspected he was keeping something back. "Do you remember that woman at the feed store?" he asked Travis, as though she'd barely caught their notice. "We wondered at the time if that little sissy truck with the out-of-state plates was hers."

Travis's expression was speculative. "The cute little blonde you tried to knock down? Of course I remember. I'm married, not dead."

"What's this?" Charlie demanded, reining his mount closer to the other two. "Why haven't I heard about her before?"

"It wasn't important," Adam said, exasperated.

"Are you telling us that she's the one who bought the Johnson place?" Travis's tone was incredulous. So much for slipping that little fact unnoticed into the conversation.

"Who is she?" Charlie asked, glancing back and forth between his two brothers, neither of whom was paying him any mind. "Would someone kindly tell me what's going on?"

"That's what I'd like to know," Travis drawled.

"Nothing's going on," Adam exclaimed. "I'm doing my best to close a business deal for the good of the Running W, just like I always do." He hadn't meant to add that last part. They were all keenly aware of what running the ranch had cost him, but it wasn't his intention to whine about it.

Travis gathered up his reins and urged his mount forward as a determined heifer broke from the group, her calf struggling to keep up with her. One of the dogs streaked past Adam, barking excitedly while Charlie headed in the other direction before the rest of the herd could follow.

Swearing under his breath, Adam prepared to join the fray before one of the animals got hurt. At least the skirmish had served one good purpose: it gave his brothers something to focus on besides Emily Major. With luck he'd have a signed deed in his pocket before the subject came up again.

The little country church with its stained-glass windows and narrow steeple poking up toward heaven belonged on a Christmas card sprinkled with silver glitter, Emily thought as she drove past the worshippers starting to head up the walkway lined in flower beds to the open front doors. Several people turned to stare as she parked her silver-blue pickup at the end of a row of freshly washed cars and trucks.

Her palms were damp on the steering wheel, and she wished that David hadn't woken up this morning with the start of a cold. Refusing to put her own need for moral support ahead of the best interest of her child, she'd sent him back to bed after breakfast and set out for church by herself. From parent-teacher conferences to Little League games, she was used to showing up alone, she reminded herself as she checked her makeup in the rearview mirror. Stuart had usually been too busy working to join her, but he'd found the time to father a half sister for David without Emily suspecting a thing.

Taking a deep breath, she got out of her truck, smoothed down the long skirt of her black-and-white polka-dotted dress, relaxed the death grip on her purse and marched across the grass with what she hoped was a pleasant expression plastered on her face. She'd planned to arrive at the last minute so she could slip into the back of the congregation unnoticed, but the drive hadn't taken as long as she'd figured.

As Emily approached the sea of strangers, a dark-haired man with a mustache glanced her way. He was carrying a little girl with bright orange curls, and something about his face looked vaguely familiar. He spoke to the woman at his side, a tall, striking redhead holding a little boy's hand. Except for the swell of her stomach, she was as willowy as a dancer. They watched Emily with welcoming smiles as though they'd been waiting to greet her.

"Welcome," the woman said. "I'm Rory Winchester, and this is my husband, Travis."

Emily's relief at the friendly overture turned to dismay when she heard their last name. Warily she glanced around, but she didn't see the man she'd initially mistaken for an overenthusiastic suitor.

"Hi, I'm Emily Major," she replied, shaking first the hand Travis Winchester extended and then his wife's. Her skin was softer than his, and without the calluses, but her grip was equally firm despite her ultrafeminine appearance.

The little girl in the crook of Travis's arm flashed Emily an impressive set of dimples.

Her eyes were the same navy blue as her mother's.

"This is Lucy, and that's our son, Steven," Travis said with a warm glance at the dark-haired boy.

"Pleased to meet you," he recited politely, his cheeks turning pink as he looked up at Emily.

Emily greeted both children. Steven ducked his head, and Lucy studied her with a child's frank stare.

"I recognized you from the feed store," Travis said. "I was with my brother when he tried to run you over in the doorway. It appears you survived."

That explained his connection to the man so determined to buy her out. Did Travis realize who she was? "As you can see, I'm still in one piece," she replied. "It's nice to meet all of you."

"Newcomers to Waterloo tend to stand out," he said. "Especially the pretty ones." His wife elbowed him playfully, and they exchanged smiles, the easy affection between them plain to see.

"Don't mind my husband," she told Emily. "Most of the locals still think of me as a newcomer, and I've lived here for five years." There was a trace of East Coast in her voice that Emily couldn't quite place. "I'm from New York," Rory added. "How about you?"

"Southern California," Emily replied as they trailed after the last of the people going inside. "I bought the Johnson place," she added, wondering whether they already knew and that was why they were being so friendly.

"Then we really are neighbors," was all she said. "Why don't you sit with us inside, and we can introduce you around afterward?"

"Thanks, that would be nice." The knot of nerves in Emily's stomach began to loosen.

"It's a shame Adam and his daughter aren't here," Rory said in an undertone as they crossed the vestibule. "He took her to Colorado Springs for the weekend to buy her a dress for the school dance."

So Emily's nemesis had a child. It seemed odd that he would be the one to take her clothes shopping, unless her mother was no longer in the picture. Despite the negative impression he'd made on Emily, it sounded as though Adam took his duties as a parent seriously. How she wished her ex-husband felt the same way.

She would have liked to ask what grade the girl was in. David hadn't said anything about a dance. Perhaps Adam's daughter attended a private school.

Emily followed Rory down the center aisle of the church, aware of the heads turning curiously and the murmured greetings when they took their places in the pew. Travis had entered first, still carrying Lucy, and Steven sat between him and Rory, with Emily on the end. Before anyone around them could do more than smile or nod, the choir filed in, followed by the minister, and the service began with a hymn.

The simple decor of the interior was complemented by the elegant tapestries on the walls, the gleam of well-polished wood and the masses of flowers Emily assumed had been provided by members of the congregation. Beeswax tapers burned on the altar. Behind it was a large, round, stained-glass window, the rich colors of its traditional biblical scene glowing as brightly as a neon sign.

At the conclusion of the hymn, the minister began to pray. Hands clasped loosely in her lap, Emily let the soothing words wash over her bowed head. Long before the service was over, she experienced the healing sense of peace and comfort that attending services nearly always brought her. Her only regret was that David wasn't here with her. He was having such a difficult time adjusting to the changes in their lives, and Emily didn't know what, if anything, she could do to help him.

Despite her concern for her son, she enjoyed the sermon, the prayers and especially the music. After the service was over and the minister had walked up the aisle past their pew, she left with Rory and her family. They seemed to know everyone. Emily met so many people on her way to the exit that she doubted she'd ever be able to keep them all straight.

When they got to the front steps, Travis introduced her to the minister. "Welcome to Waterloo," Reverend Foley boomed as he pumped Emily's hand. With his rotund build and fringe of hair, all he needed were brown robes and sandals to pass for a Franciscan monk. "Do you have family around here?"

"Not a soul," Emily replied. "My son, David, and I needed a change of pace, and I fell for Colorado when I got off the plane in Denver." She didn't add that she'd come to scout out Ed Johnson's property, nor did she figure it would be polite to mention that David thought the locals were a bunch of hayseeds. "He's home with a cold," she said instead.

"I hope you'll bring him with you next Sunday," the minister replied. "Meanwhile, if there's anything my wife or I can do to help you settle in, don't hesitate to call. Rosemary will be disappointed that she missed meeting you, but she's off to Cheyenne to visit her sister until midweek."

"I hope you'll join us for dinner one evening while you're batching it," Rory told him. With her approval, Steven had gone with another little boy down to the lawn for a game of tag. He reminded Emily so much of David at that age. Life had been much simpler then.

The minister's smile widened in response to Rory's invitation. "Rosemary left me a couple of frozen casseroles with detailed instructions, but I have to admit that eating alone isn't much fun." He leaned closer. "You know how fond I am of your cooking," he added conspiratorially. "Just don't tell my wife that I prefer your meat loaf to hers."

"Or that you're a shameless flatterer," Rory responded, glancing at the line waiting to greet him. "Come tomorrow, and I might just whip up that dinner you like."

"With mashed potatoes?" he asked hopefully.

"Of course."

The minister's pleased expression faded as he glanced discreetly at Rory's rounded stomach. "It won't be too much trouble?"

Travis curved his free arm around his wife's shoulders. "I've tried to get her to slow down," he said, "but she's stubborn. Must be all that red hair."

"Compared to slinging hash for a diner full of customers, feeding one family and the occasional guest is child's play," she exclaimed, piquing Emily's curiosity. "We'll look for you tomorrow, Reverend."

After he'd promised to be there, he excused himself to greet another parishioner, and Travis guided Rory down the front steps as carefully as if he were escorting royalty.

"Would you and your son like to join us?" she asked Emily when they reached the sidewalk where knots of people stood visiting. "We'd love to meet him."

Emily was touched by the easy way the invitation was issued, as though they were already friends. Although that might not be possible, Emily liked the idea. "Might I take a rain check until my son is over his cold?" she asked regretfully.

"Sure thing. Let's make it soon, though. We're neighbors, after all." Rory's smile was guileless as she reached into her purse and extracted a card she handed Emily. "Here's my number. In the meantime, at least come by for coffee some morning."

Emily thanked her and tucked the card in her pocket, intending to slip away quietly. Her plans were thwarted when Rory led her to another group and began making introductions.

"Don't even try to keep everyone straight," she told Emily between names. "If you're anything like me, all these new faces will be a blur for a good while yet, but at least it's a start." She winked at Emily. "Besides, they're all curious as heck about why you would move here from southern California, when the change has to be like crash landing on a different planet. Everyone's just too polite to ask."

Emily sensed that asking was just what Rory was doing. What would she say if Emily told her she'd brought her son here to save his life and that she had no intention of selling their new home, not to anyone?

Now wasn't the time for confidences, especially with someone whose last name began with a *W.* Emily settled for part of the truth. "I wanted David to attend a school that didn't need metal detectors and armed guards patrolling the halls."

"I'm afraid that day will come, even here," Rory replied regretfully. "We're lucky that so far we've had no trouble. It's very different from the Bronx, where I grew up."

"Why did you pick Waterloo?" Emily asked curiously. "Did you already know Travis?"

Rory glanced at her husband, who was talking to an older man with a face like tanned leather and a bolo tie with a turquoise stone the size and color of a robin's egg tucked beneath the folds of his chin. "Do you remember that attractive hunk in the choir who sang the solo this morning?" she asked Emily.

"Of course. How could I not? He had a wonderful voice." And looks to match, she thought. For a small town, Waterloo had more than its share of attractive men.

"That was Charlie, Adam and Travis's younger brother." Rory looked around. "He must have ducked out right after the service, probably has a hot date, knowing him. Anyway, he was the first Winchester I met, but that's a story best told over coffee."

Emily absorbed the information silently as a little girl who looked to be the same age as Steven asked Rory where he'd gone. She pointed out her son, and the child ran off.

"I understand you've already met Adam," Rory said to Emily.

"Yes, I have." She was tempted to add more, but since the man was Rory's brother-in-law, she restrained herself.

"He's trying to buy you out."

Her bluntness surprised Emily, who decided to be blunt in return. "He's been by a couple of times, but I'm not selling. We just got here."

Rory tossed her head, sending her apricot curls flying. "Good for you. Not getting what he wants will build Adam's character." Her smile flashed. "Honey, everyone in the county knows how much he covets your land, but what you decide to do is your business. It doesn't mean you and I can't be friends."

Emily returned her smile. "Thank you. He warned me he'd be back." She remembered his determination and suppressed a shiver.

"Oh, he will." Rory leaned closer, her eyes brimming with laughter. "I don't see a husband in tow, and you aren't wearing a ring. Does that mean you're single?"

The forthright question caught Emily off guard. "Divorced."

"Ah." Rory's grin turned smug. "Don't let Adam push you around. He's had it tough, and he can be a little intimidating, but he's as honorable as any man in the county."

Emily wasn't sure how to reply. "I'm sure he is," she said finally, "but I'm still not selling."

Rory chuckled. "I understand. The character reference I was giving Adam was a personal one." Her gaze strayed to her spouse. "Winchester men make good husbands."

"He's not interested in me that way," Emily protested, slightly horrified at the idea. "I'm not in the market for a husband or anything else involving a man, honorable or otherwise. All I want is to put down a few roots and provide a peaceful home for my son."

Rory's gaze was steady, giving Emily the impression that the other woman could see past her words to the feelings behind them. Rory's expression softened slightly. "I understand what you're saying. You just keep standing up to Adam," she said enigmatically. "You'll be fine."

Before Emily could think of a response, Steven ran up and tugged on Rory's skirt. "Mommy," he whispered loudly, "I have to go potty right now!"

She put her hand on his dark head before she turned back to Emily. "I hope you will come by for coffee."

"I'll try." Perhaps a visit wouldn't be a good idea if it meant running into Adam again. "Thanks for everything."

"No problem. I know what it's like to be the new kid on the block."

After Rory excused herself and allowed Steven to tow her away, Emily waved goodbye to Travis, who smiled in response. Before anyone else could approach her, she headed toward the parking area.

Adam took one look at the midriff-baring black outfit his daughter had on as she left the dressing room and decided he was being set up. Kim probably figured he'd happily double the limit he'd allowed if she would agree to something that covered more skin than it bared. "Okay, you've had your little joke," he said with a grin. "Now show me the dress you really want, so we can get some lunch and head home. It's a long drive, and I've got paperwork waiting."

"Daddy!" she wailed, surprising him. "This *is* what I want. It's just what everyone else will be wearing."

"Everyone but you," he replied firmly, trying not to notice the amount of leg the tiny skirt revealed. Even with her lip poked out and her blue eyes filling with angry tears, she was growing up before his eyes. "Now find something that makes you look like a fifteen-year-old and not a dance-hall girl."

"I don't think they sell nun's habits here," she retorted.

He kept his expression blank. "Well, you've

probably got something in your closet that
would do."

She spun around and stomped back into
the fitting room, her long, dark hair swirling
like silk. Adam stifled a chuckle. Two could
play that game.

When she came out a few minutes later,
still pouting, his heart stuttered in his chest.
She was wearing a simple blue dress that
matched her eyes. It was shorter than he
would have liked, but he knew he'd buy it if
she wanted. Then he'd chaperone that dance
with a baseball bat tucked behind him, just
in case.

Emily was in her studio the next morning
with a cup of coffee in hand and the fragile old Bible on her worktable, when Monty,
who'd been curled up by the heater, raised his
head and whined.

Emily pushed her chair back. Her neck was
stiff from studying the Bible through the big
magnifying glass. She glanced at the collie,
who'd gotten to his feet. "What is it, boy?"

As Monty padded over to the door, Emily
heard the sound of an approaching vehicle.
Her first thought was that Adam was back
and the only concession she'd made to her appearance this morning was to wind her hair

into a topknot and stick a pencil through it. Her second thought was to wonder why it mattered.

A quick peek through the window revealed an older model Chrysler in vintage condition with a ton of chrome and wide whitewall tires. Two elderly women were in the car, the driver barely tall enough to see over the steering wheel. While Emily watched, she parked the sedan as carefully as if she were docking a cruise ship. Chatting happily, the two women got out, each dressed in colorful sweats and matching jackets, one purple and one bright pink. Emily remembered her visitors from church the day before, even though they'd been wearing flowered dresses and straw hats. Now one carried a pie-shaped plastic container and the other, the driver, held a bouquet of mixed flowers as they went up the porch steps.

Patting her hair to make sure it was secure, Emily opened the door of her studio as she filed a mental note to hang up a small mirror. Monty ran ahead of her, tail wagging, and she had a sudden image of him knocking over her frail visitors like bowling pins. She called sharply, and he skidded to a stop, tongue lolling as he glanced back at her as if to say, *Give me a little credit.*

The women both turned at the sound of her voice. "Hello," the one in pink called out cheerfully. "I'm Bonnie Price, and this is Violet MacAffee. We met yesterday morning. We just dropped by to welcome you to the area."

"I brought you a pie," the other woman said, holding up the container. "I hope you like apple."

"It's one of my very favorites," Emily replied as she joined them, grateful to be reminded of their names. "Won't you come in? I'll make some coffee."

"Don't let us take you away from whatever you were doing," Bonnie said, peering curiously at the studio. "We can come back some other day if you're busy."

"Actually, I could use a break." Emily realized she was telling the truth. She'd been hunched over the old Bible since David had left for school, the piece of toast she'd fixed forgotten at her elbow.

Emily led the way inside, aware of the women's interested glances. They'd probably known Mr. Johnson, since they appeared to be from the same generation. Rory had mentioned yesterday that they were both widows, so they might even have competed in a friendly way for his attention.

After Emily had invited them both to sit

down in the dining room, she put the flowers into a vase and set it on the table. While the coffee was brewing, she cut through the flaky crust of the pie.

"You've fixed the house up real nice," Violet said. "I heard the previous owner went to live with a relative."

"That's what he told me he was planning," Emily said as she set out milk and sugar. "I don't think he cared to live alone anymore."

The two women exchanged glances. "It was all so sudden," Bonnie said as Emily set a piece of pie in front of her. "No one knew he was selling."

"I saw the ad on an Internet listing," Emily volunteered after she'd checked on the coffee. "It sounded like just what I was looking for, so I flew out from California right away." Briefly she described her business and mentioned David. By then the coffee was ready.

"Did Mr. Johnson tell you why he didn't advertise locally?" Violet asked, her eyes bright with interest behind her thick glasses. "Everyone thought the Winchesters would buy him out whenever he was ready."

Emily decided not to mention Adam's visits or the promise she'd made Mr. Johnson. "I have no idea what his motives were," she said truthfully. "This pie is wonderful. Bonnie, are the flowers from your garden?"

Her visitors glanced at each other, but they went along with the change of subject. Violet told Emily how many blue ribbons her pies had won at the county fair, and Bonnie invited her to join the local garden club. Emily braced herself for more probing questions, but the two women seemed content to pass on snippets of gossip about her neighbors.

"Of course you met Travis and his lovely little family yesterday," Bonnie said after she'd finished her coffee and turned down the offer of a refill. "Did Rory happen to mention that both of his brothers are unattached?"

Emily felt her cheeks turn pink. "I don't remember if that came up." She glanced down at her cup, wondering if she should warn them that she hadn't moved to Colorado to find a man. If they were matchmaking, they were wasting their time.

"How old are you, dear?" Bonnie asked before she could decide.

"I'm thirty-three."

"Probably a little too old for Charlie," Violet mused. Her frankness nearly made Emily laugh out loud. "He's got a wandering eye, anyway." Violet made a dismissive gesture with her hand. "Adam's much more settled."

"Too settled if you ask me," Bonnie replied. "All the man seems to care about is that ranch the family owns."

"But he's a good father to his little girl," Violet said. "Ever since her mother ran off and left him, he's had to be both parents to her."

For a moment Emily struggled between the reluctance to indulge in gossip that was really none of her business and curiosity about the man to whom she felt a grudging and unwanted attraction. An attraction these old dears would sniff out like bloodhounds. Prudence won out, and Emily sneaked a glance at her watch.

The women noticed, just as she knew they would, and Bonnie pushed back her chair. "We've taken up enough of your time," she said briskly. "Thank you for the coffee, but we've got a few errands to run before bingo."

Looking much more reluctant, Violet set aside her napkin.

"Don't let me rush you," Emily said politely. "My work will be waiting for me whenever I get back to it." She thanked them again for the pie and the flowers, and they both invited her to return their visit in the near future.

Moments later Emily watched them disappear down the driveway in the grand old

Chrysler. She was about to go back to the studio when the phone rang.

Who would be calling her here? As any mother would, she thought immediately of David and the school. As she hurried into the house, the memory of another call from another school rose up in her throat like bile, threatening to gag her.

Chapter Four

Emily lifted the receiver with fingers that trembled. Normally she wasn't so nervous, but she worried about her son's welfare and dreaded hearing bad news from his school.

As soon as she'd said hello and heard the familiar voice on the other end of the line, she sagged with a relief that was immediately chased away by annoyance.

"Stuart! What do you want?" she demanded, not caring whether she sounded rude. The fact that he'd left Emily for another woman had long since ceased to matter to her, but what she would not forgive was the indifferent way he treated David.

"Not even a simple how-are-you?" He was

using his professional tone, the one that revealed not a trace of emotion.

"How are you, Stuart?" she replied evenly. "How's the family? How's work? How's—"

"Never mind," he cut in sharply. "I get your drift."

Emily smiled to herself, childishly pleased she'd managed to irk him. Her hand tightened on the receiver as she reminded herself that if she provoked him too much, he was liable to take his annoyance out on their son. Still, she couldn't force herself to apologize. Instead she merely waited.

Stuart drew in an audible breath, and she could picture his expression as clearly as if he'd been glaring at her across the room. His disapproval would be evident in the slight curl to his lip and the narrowing of his eyes. When they'd been married, she had tried hard to please him, but she could never quite manage it. For a moment she nearly resented their one last tie, but she couldn't very well blame David for his parentage.

"I see that you haven't changed a bit." The icy control was back in Stuart's voice. "You're just as difficult to deal with as you always were. What is it you want from me, Emily? As hard as I tried to make you happy, I was never able to figure out what you expected."

Sudden fury engulfed her. Throughout their marriage, she had knocked herself out to please the man, with little recognition and even less success. The idea that he'd put himself out for her was laughable.

Now it was her turn to draw in a shaky breath. "This is pointless. If the only reason you called was to rehash my shortcomings, I'm going to hang up."

"Wait!" His demanding tone set her teeth on edge. Why did she let him get to her like this? Her stomach was in a knot, she was trembling, and tears of frustration filled her eyes.

"What is it?" she snapped, no longer caring that he knew he'd upset her. She'd never be completely free as long as she allowed his opinion of her to matter.

"I called to speak to our son. Would you please summon him to the phone?"

Emily glanced at the little porcelain clock on the mantel with incredulity. "He's not here," she exclaimed. "I know it's been a while since you've talked to David, but don't tell me you've forgotten that he's still a high school student." Oh, but the sarcasm she allowed to seep into her voice felt good!

"Tell him I called."

Before she could respond, there was a sharp

click as Stuart hung up. Feeling worlds better that she'd gotten in a dig, Emily replaced the receiver and dashed the tears from her eyes.

Almost immediately her glee was replaced with regret. David was bound to be disappointed that he had missed his father's call, especially when she fibbed and told him it had come right before he got home this afternoon. She wanted to shield him from the extent of Stuart's self-absorption.

Since the morning was shot as far as getting any work done, and she wasn't nearly calm enough to tackle the kind of detail her current projects demanded, Emily decided to finish setting out the bedding plants she'd stopped to buy on her way home from church the day before. Digging in the dirt always soothed her jangled nerves. She and David had spent the previous afternoon weeding the existing garden, but there were still several flats of annuals that needed to go into the beds they'd prepared along the sidewalk and in front of the porch. Emily could hardly wait for the red and white petunias, the sapphire-blue lobelia and the bright yellow marigolds to bloom, filling the yard with color.

When she was finally done tucking her plants into the soil, she stood back to admire her work and then she headed for the coolness of the stable.

Monty was sound asleep in the tall grass beneath a cottonwood tree, his stomach rising and falling with reassuring regularity, so she was careful not to disturb him. When she got to the stable, she pushed open the door and stepped inside. A wide aisle ran the length of the interior with two roomy stalls on each side. At the far end was an open area with running water and a drain in the floor, opposite a storage room big enough for feed and tack. Since she'd cleaned the area, an ambitious spider had spun a web at the juncture of one post and a crossbeam. Dust motes floated in the light from a window.

Emily sat down on a wooden chest in front of the largest stall and leaned back against the door, willing herself to forget about her ex-husband and concentrate instead on the future she was carving out for herself and her son. As she closed her eyes and tried to relax, she could almost hear the echoes of clopping hooves and soft whinnies. A faint earthy smell lingered in the air, reminding her how much she had missed being around horses.

Mr. Johnson had told her he'd kept a couple of head until a few years ago, but his only

recent boarders had been barn cats. A friend
of his had taken them in after the sale. Even
though mice and snakes didn't bother Emily,
she would probably need a cat or two to keep
the rodent population manageable. Rats liked
to eat the paper she used in her studio, and
they could inflict a great deal of damage to
the irreplaceable tomes entrusted to her. To
her mental list of things to do in the very
near future she added a trip to the local animal shelter.

A meow interrupted her thoughts. Just as
she realized the sound was too close and too
insistent to be a product of her imagination,
something soft butted against her leg.

Emily's eyes popped open, and she looked
down to see a calico cat staring back at her.
Its face was equally divided, half black and
half white, its eyes were as round and as copper as pennies. It was rather small except for
its bulging sides. The poor thing wore no collar, but it was very pregnant and probably
hungry.

Cautiously Emily extended her hand, half
expecting the creature to bolt. After a polite
sniff, it rubbed against her fingers, and she
could hear a loud but ragged rumble. Talking
nonsense, Emily stroked its head and back,

deciding to call the cat Penny because of the color and shape of its eyes.

Judging from Penny's condition, Emily's barn-cat problem was more than solved. As soon as she gave birth, a trip to the vet was in order. There were too many unwanted kittens in the world for Emily to condone indiscriminate breeding. Meanwhile, until she could get to the store and buy cat food, canned tuna would have to suffice.

Early the next morning, Monty's raucous barking woke Emily from a sound sleep. Prying open her eyelids, she glanced at the clock on her nightstand and groaned. The room was light, but it was still too early to get up. The dog usually slept in David's room, and so far Monty had been quiet unless he heard a suspicious noise. Could someone be prowling around outside?

"Mom?" David knocked softly on her door. "Are you awake?" He'd been disappointed about his father's call the day before, especially since Emily let him believe he'd only missed it by a half hour and not half a day. He'd insisted on phoning Stuart back right away, but his father was no homebody. He'd been on the golf course with a client.

"Yes, honey, I'm up." Emily got out of bed

and pulled on her robe. "What's got Monty so upset? Are you okay?"

"He woke me up," David said through the closed door as she rooted around under her bed for her slippers. "I'm going to check around outside."

She gave up on the slippers. What if an intruder *was* snooping around? "David!" she cried, getting to her feet. "You stay in the house."

Before she could get to the bedroom door, it opened a crack, and her son peered at her.

"Mom," he said, "look out your window. The yard is full of cows."

Adam inspected the break in the fence, noted the direction in which the path of trampled grass pointed and swore under his breath. For the past few days he'd been too busy rounding up strays to pay another visit to Ms. Major, but it looked as though fate had just intervened. He'd have to tell her about the section of fence that was down and find out what she planned to do about having it repaired.

Adam had stayed up late the night before doing paperwork, and he'd gotten up at dawn this morning to ride out with the men. The area they were covering today was too uneven for a Jeep to be practical, which suited him just fine. If he could, he would have done all his work from the back of a horse, including the accounts.

When it had become evident the cattle they were trailing had scattered, he'd sent Barney one way, and he'd gone another.

For once the natural beauty of the area was lost on Adam as he debated riding back for help or dealing with the situation by himself. When both dogs had followed after Barney, Adam should have whistled one back, but he hadn't bothered. There was no help for it now. If he couldn't manage to drive a half dozen head back onto Winchester land, perhaps it was time to hang up his spurs and ride a desk full-time.

"Get out of my flowers," Emily wailed. After one horrified glance through her bedroom window, she'd thrown on the first clothes she could grab and rushed outside with David on her heels. The moment she'd opened the door, Monty raced by them, barking wildly as he charged the black, tan and white cows—each paired with a calf Emily would have thought cute under other circumstances.

Her aging collie was attempting to herd

them, but so far he'd only succeeding in making them nervous. The cows rolled their big brown eyes as they shifted one way and then another, calves bawling, hooves trampling more plants with every step.

Emily didn't have the vaguest idea how to get the dog to move the cattle out of the garden. Instead she advanced on the huge beasts warily, waving her arms and shouting. A couple of them, each twice as big as a chest freezer, lifted their heads to watch her curiously, but they appeared as uncertain of what to do as Emily.

"I bet I could round them up on my bike," David suggested hopefully.

She turned to glare at him. "I have enough to worry about without watching you get mashed into the dirt like an overripe banana," she snapped, pushing the hair she hadn't taken the time to secure out of her eyes.

The wind kept blowing it across her face and goose bumps had popped up her bare arms like hives. In true Colorado fashion, the temperature had dropped significantly since yesterday. Maybe the man at the nursery had been right in suggesting she wait a couple of weeks to do her planting, but the sunshine had fooled her, and she'd been eager to see the flowers in bloom.

Not that it mattered now!

"The noise from the bike would probably stampede them," she added for her son's benefit. "We don't need that."

"Like your screeching and flapping your arms is calming them down," he muttered just loud enough for her to hear.

Emily ignored him as a tan cow standing on the sidewalk lifted its tail and left a large deposit on the cement. Its hide bore a slanted *W* brand.

Emily narrowed her eyes. Adam Winchester had a lot to answer for. Not only had her hard work from the day before been ground into the dirt, but the rough lawn surrounding the house was torn up, as well. If he thought a few cows would drive her out, he was mistaken.

"Open the corral gate and then help me get them out of the garden," she told her son. "After we get them contained, I'll call someone from the neighboring ranch."

"I'm not going to run around like an idiot making stupid noises," David exclaimed. "Besides, what if they go out on the main road instead of where you want them? They could cause a wreck. Maybe I should call the sheriff."

Emily swallowed her irritation at David's

concern with his image. Who was here to see him except her? "What do you think the sheriff is going to do, arrest them?" Taking a deep breath, she approached the intruders warily.

"Shoo, shoo!" she shouted, waving her arms. A little spotted calf darted behind its mother, bawling pitifully, but none of the adults moved. A black cow with a white face lowered its head and nibbled on a row of early peas. Had they knocked over the fence or wandered up the driveway? Was there a chance one of them might charge her or did only bulls do that? They didn't look terribly aggressive, and only a couple of them had horns, she realized. Perhaps if Emily called Rory, she'd send Travis over to collect them.

Monty had stopped running. He dropped to his belly, tongue lolling out as he watched Emily with his ears pricked, but she didn't know the command for "round up these danged cows and coax them into the corral before they all poop on the lawn."

Suddenly one white cow with lethal-looking horns broke away from the group, lowered its head and came right at her. With a screech of fright, Emily ran for the safety of the porch. Grabbing the railing, she bounded up the steps two at a time and nearly collided with David, who'd been standing at the top of the stairs. As she whirled around to make sure the white cow hadn't followed her, heart banging like a drum, a whoop of laughter nearly froze her blood.

Masculine laughter.

Adam Winchester was sitting on a horse in her driveway, nearly bent double over the saddle horn as his shoulders shook with mirth. As he struggled to squelch his amusement with limited success, he lifted his head. His sea-green gaze collided with Emily's.

Any relief she might have felt that help had arrived was blotted out by the realization of how ridiculous her headlong flight for safety—from a cow!—must have looked to the rancher. If she hadn't been so angry and humiliated, she might have been stunned by the devastating change his outburst had wrought on his normally serious expression. Instead his laughter at her expense only whipped the flames of her temper into a full-fledged inferno.

"Look what your animals have done to my flowers," she raged, pointing her finger accusingly as his grin finally faded. "You get those walking hamburger patties off my land right now!"

As he urged his horse closer to the porch, she charged back down the steps she'd so recently ascended. The necessity of having to tip back her head to look at him, seated tall in the saddle with merriment still dancing in his eyes only added to her irritation. The man's sense of humor was ill placed and perverse.

"Well, what are you waiting for?" she demanded when he didn't immediately whip out a lasso and round up his livestock. "Do I need to call the sheriff?"

The attractive Appaloosa that Adam was riding sidestepped, its ears flicking back and forth in silent disapproval of Emily's strident tone. Patting his mount's neck with a gloved hand, Adam spoke soothingly until it quieted.

"It takes a lot to spook old Zeke," he observed in the same mild voice. "No reason to bother Sheriff Hathaway about this. I'm sorry my cattle escaped."

The inadequacy of his apology and his patronizing tone, on top of his failure to contain his amusement at her expense, had Emily teetering on the edge of her control. If she had been considering selling to him, which she hadn't, she would have changed her mind out of sheer spite. Not only had his stock trampled her garden, but there was at least one large cow patty that needed hosing off her sidewalk.

"I'll just run them back through that break

in the fence," Adam said, jabbing his thumb in the direction from which he'd come. He'd barely glanced at the damage to her yard.

"What are you going to do about this mess?" She knew she sounded like a shrew and probably looked like Medusa with strands of hair blowing around her face in the stiff breeze, but she refused to care what he might think of her appearance. She was not, after all, interested in him that way—or any way, except perhaps as a target were she ever to take up shooting. "Who's going to replace all my ruined flowers and vegetables?"

Leaning down, he rested his folded arms on the saddle horn and studied her through narrowed eyes. "Who do you think should replace them?"

Emily parked her hands on her hips and glared. Part of her anger, she realized, stemmed from his unfair advantage. While she must look as if she shopped at the local thrift store, he could have posed for a Colorado hunks calendar. He hadn't shaved this morning and dark whiskers traced the line of his jaw, but what should have looked scruffy added an element of danger to his appearance. His jet-black hair brushed the turned-up collar of his denim jacket, and scarred leather chaps hugged his muscular legs.

She refused to be distracted from the problem at hand. "They're your cattle," she pointed out with a sniff.

He started to say something, but then he shrugged instead, drawing her attention to his broad shoulders. The sardonic twist of his mouth was mirrored in the arrogant lift of his brows.

"Why don't you just sell me your land?" he suggested with outrageous brass. "Then you won't have to worry about your garden. I can't imagine why you bothered planting it when you won't be here long enough to see it produce."

"I like growing things," she replied through gritted teeth as an ugly suspicion formed in her mind. She was about to ask whether he had deliberately let his cattle wander onto her property when she saw that his attention had shifted. She'd nearly forgotten about David, who'd been watching their heated exchange from the porch.

"Good Lord, who's that?" Adam blurted, staring.

Emily didn't care for his tone. She looked at her son through her neighbor's eyes, his dark hair bleached to a bright shade of orange on top and shaved close on the sides, the row of small gold hoops in his ear catching the sunlight. He'd pulled on an orange-and-purple bowling shirt he'd bought in a vintage clothing shop back in L.A., paired with oversize tan shorts and unlaced combat boots with no socks. To an undoubtedly traditional rancher like Adam, David must have looked rather bizarre. Emily had grown so used to his unique appearance that she barely noticed until someone else's reaction reminded her.

"This is my son, David," she said now. "David, this is Mr. Winchester, our nearest neighbor and the owner of our other visitors."

David stepped forward and mumbled a greeting, hands jammed in his deep pockets, while Adam tipped his hat without smiling. Hostility crackled in the air between the two males, puzzling Emily.

"You'd better get ready for school, honey," she said. "I'll be there in a minute to fix breakfast."

"I'll just get my cattle out of your way," the rancher told her, uncoiling his rope after David had gone back inside with obvious reluctance.

"What about my flowers?" she reminded the man as she shifted around in front of his horse before he could ride off. "Who's going to pay for replacements?"

"Make a list," he said shortly. "I'll send someone by to pick it up later."

As Adam drove the cattle back onto Winchester property, he wondered why he hadn't just informed his irritating new neighbor that the section of fence that had been breached was her responsibility and not that of the Running W. Instead of placing blame for the break right where it belonged—squarely on her feminine shoulders—he'd allowed himself to become distracted by the sight of all that blonde hair tumbling around her face as though she'd just climbed out of bed. The temper sparkling in her dark eyes made him wonder if she was as passionate about everything as she was her flowers.

Was there a man in her life? Adam hadn't seen any sign of one. She had a son, but the deed to the property referred to her as an unmarried woman.

The image of her in that white T-shirt kept rising up in Adam's mind, distracting him. She must have dressed in a hurry because she hadn't been wearing a bra, and her nipples had puckered like lemon drops in the chill breeze. Too bad her son caught Adam gawking like a greenhorn at a stampede.

That boy of hers looked like trouble. Adam was tempted to warn his daughter away from him, but Kim was a sensible girl who didn't need to be told that Mr. California was someone to avoid—despite her earlier comment about him.

Maybe Adam himself was the one who needed the warning. One destructive blonde in a man's life was enough.

"Do you know anything about flowers?" Emily asked Cody, the young cowhand who had shown up at her door with a wad of gum in his cheek. He'd tipped his hat politely, introduced himself and called her ma'am, which made her feel like a senior citizen as she handed him a list of the plants that needed replacing.

It was only the middle of the afternoon, and David was still at school. She hadn't expected anyone to show up so promptly. In truth, she'd figured her neighbor would forget all about it, so she'd planned on buying replacements herself and sending the bill to the Running W. Now she ignored the sharp little niggle of disappointment that he hadn't come back in person. He was probably too busy running his empire and chasing strays to concern himself with a piddling little chore like this one.

"Yes, ma'am, my mother plants a lot of flowers, too," Cody replied, his cheeks turning a fiery shade of red. He appeared to be only a few years older than David, but any similarity between the boys stopped there. In his Western hat, striped shirt and faded Wranglers, Cody looked like exactly what he was, a working cowboy.

Glancing over his shoulder as if to make sure no one overheard, he added, "I like to help her, so I've had a fair amount of practice picking them out." He scanned the list. "Pansies, petunias, marigolds, lobelia, snapdragons," he muttered aloud. "No problem. Have you thought about planting sunflowers? A row of them would be great along the edge of your vegetable patch."

Emily turned to study the area. "Good idea," she replied. "I'll look for some seeds the next time I go to town."

"No need," he replied. "I'll pick them up today. Adam told me to buy whatever it takes to make you happy."

Emily didn't bother to hide her surprise. "Really?" The man must be feeling extremely guilty. Perhaps there was a fine for letting your cattle run loose, and he didn't want her reporting him to the sheriff.

"I'll be back first thing in the morning to plant them, if that's all right with you," Cody promised.

"That would be fine." Emily walked him back to his dusty dark green pickup with its oversize tires. "I hope this isn't taking you away from your regular duties."

His grin flashed white. "It's a nice break from looking for critters that don't appreciate being found."

"I suppose so," she agreed absently. It wasn't Cody she pictured riding flat-out across the plains in hot pursuit of a stray cow, but his boss. Tempted to ask Cody what Adam was like to work for, she thanked the young ranch hand instead and watched him drive away.

She hadn't dragged her son to Colorado in search of complications but to escape them, she reminded herself grimly. The only thing Adam Winchester wanted from Emily was the land she stood on, and she had no idea how far he was willing to go in order to obtain it. She'd had her fill of bossy men. Any attraction she might feel toward the arrogant rancher was definitely a complication she could do without.

Chapter Five

Bouncing down Ms. Major's driveway with a pickup load of bedding plants, Adam tried not to think about all the work waiting for him back at his own ranch. It wasn't any use telling himself his motivation in coming here was persuading her to sell—not with the vision of her in that white T-shirt crowding his common sense like a randy bull calf.

Adam could still picture the surprise on Travis's face when, right in the middle of this morning's discussion about the day's activities, Adam had announced that he had an errand in town. He'd promised to join up with the others after lunch. Although Charlie and Travis were full partners in the Running W,

Adam was the boss. He'd taken over when the old man died and technically he could do as he pleased, but usually his responsibilities to the ranch came ahead of everything except his daughter.

His time would be better spent getting his head examined, he thought now as he eased the pickup around a rut in the road. Since he hadn't been capable of telling his irritating neighbor that replacing her damn posies wasn't a Winchester responsibility, he should have at least sent Cody back to finish the chore.

Adam ought to be spending his time and brain power, what little he had of either, trying to figure out how to persuade Emily to sell him the land. Instead he seemed to be entertaining the notion that her sticking around might not be so bad after all. Somewhere between sucking in her scent and getting caught in that tumble of blonde hair, he'd lost sight of what was best for the family business and his own peace of mind.

Maybe while he was grubbing in her garden he'd remember the damage a city woman could do to the heart of a man with dirt under his nails and ranching in his blood. Had he forgotten the painful lesson he'd learned from Christie, who'd left him with a toddler in diapers and his pride in tatters? He'd sworn that he'd never need a refresher course, yet here he was with his hat in hand and his damn tongue hanging out.

Emily must have heard him coming up the drive, because she came out of the shed as he pulled up next to her fancy toy truck. He turned off the engine and jammed his new Resistol back on his head, swallowing hard. Her eyes widened behind the silly wire glasses perched on her nose. Whipping them off, she tucked them into her blouse pocket.

Hoping she might be wearing another T-shirt had proved futile on his part. Her blouse, in a shade of pink that looked good enough to lick, was tucked into faded black jeans that skimmed down her nicely rounded hips.

The lean length of denim made him curious about the shape of her legs, nearly causing him to forget that she was an obstacle and nothing more. The sooner she was off the property and out of his life, the better he'd be.

But he'd sure like a glimpse of those legs before she left town.

"I brought your flowers." His voice was gruff as he climbed out of the truck and slammed the door with unnecessary force.

Serve him right if the window busted out of spite. Barely glancing in Emily's direction, he walked past her and dropped open the tailgate.

She shot him a cautious look before she peered over the side of the box. "Looks like you bought out the nursery's entire stock," she said. "Where's Cody?"

"He's busy today." The young ranch hand was a mite green for her, Adam thought nastily. "You're stuck with me."

She ignored his comment. "I think he was a little embarrassed that he'd admitted to helping his mother with her garden," she said instead.

Adam merely raised his eyebrows as he shifted the flats around.

"What's the matter, isn't planting flowers an approved cowboy activity?" she asked in a teasing voice.

Adam knew she was goading him, but that didn't stop his reply. "Well, normally we're way too busy scratching and spitting to mess with girlie stuff like planting flowers," he drawled.

Her sudden peal of laughter made it hard to keep his poker face intact as he donned his gloves and picked up a tray of little plants with spiky dark-green leaves. Marigold, the tag said. The picture reminded him of the color of Emily's hair, a cross between sunshine and sweet butter. Today she had it secured on top of her head with a pencil poking through, like a knitting needle in a ball of yarn. He was tempted to tug on the pencil just to see if the hair would come tumbling down around her face.

"Where do you want these?" he demanded instead, gripping the flat tighter.

Her eyebrows rose, but she didn't comment on the shift in his tone. "Over by the porch will be fine," she said. "Are you sure you've got time for this, Mr. Winchester?"

Embarrassed at his own churlishness, Adam stopped and looked her full in the face. Replacing her plants had been his choice. The least he could do was drag up some manners while he was carrying out the chore.

"Call me Adam. And despite what I said about that whole cowboy thing, this does make a nice change from working cattle."

"Funny," she mused as she grabbed a flat of hot-colored zinnias and hurried after him, "Cody said nearly the same thing. Don't any of you men actually *like* cows?"

"Cattle," Adam corrected her absently. His stock had ripped up her grass some, he noticed, but the lawn would turn brown soon enough, anyway, so the damage hardly seemed important.

"Isn't that what I said?" She almost had to skip to keep up with his long stride.

"You called them cows," he explained.

"Ah, that I did. I'll try to watch it." The humor bubbled up in her voice again, making him wonder if she found him that entertaining or was starved for company—even his—stuck out here in the wilds of Colorado.

Had she made any friends yet? He knew a few single cowhands, and probably a couple of married ones, who'd come sniffing around once they got wind of her presence. Adam figured there was already plenty of talk and speculation in town about her and that son of hers.

"I noticed the plates on your truck," he said. "You're a long way from home."

Her smile faded and her gaze shifted to the bedding plants. "I was more than ready for a change," she replied, her voice subdued as she bent down to flick a jagged leaf with her finger. Her hands, he noticed, were fine-boned, her nails neatly trimmed and naked of polish. The only adornment was a gold ring set with a pearl on her right hand.

Her comment aroused his curiosity. Had he jumped to conclusions, assuming she'd bought the Johnson spread to annoy him—and to jack up the price before she sold it to him? "Well, moving here must feel like a big change." He glanced at the emptiness spreading out in every direction. Not a skyscraper in sight.

"That's true," she admitted, "but we're adjusting."

"How's your boy like the local school?" He didn't envy the kid trying to fit in. Adam had grown up in these parts and gone all through school with the same bunch of kids. He'd been one of them, until the talk after his mother took off made him feel like a freak.

"He's adapting," she said.

Adam didn't normally do a lot of prying, but his curiosity egged him on. "What about his father? Is he back in California?"

Emily nodded, not appearing to mind the personal question. "We're divorced. David misses his dad a lot."

Adam felt a surge of sympathy for the poor guy. If Christie had taken Kim out of state, it would have damn near killed him. "A boy needs his father."

She jerked her chin up and her eyes flashed. "Do I detect a note of criticism in that comment?"

Wow, he'd hit her hot button for sure. "I

don't know enough about your situation to criticize," he replied with a shrug, wishing he'd kept his damn mouth shut.

Angry color flooded her cheeks. "Not that it's any of your business, but I didn't exactly tear my son from his father's loving arms. Stuart has a new family now. He barely has time to return David's phone calls."

So her ex had remarried. Was the bitter edge to Emily's voice on her son's behalf or her own? Adam wasn't about to ask. He didn't want to know, and it wasn't his business.

"You're right," he agreed. "Why you came here isn't my concern. What's it going to take to get you off this particular twenty acres?" He ignored her outraged gasp. "Have you come down on your price yet? A million dollars seems a mite steep, considering I'm your only buyer and I'm not planning to build a supermall on the site."

She tossed her head, but her indignant expression had faded. It wasn't as though he hadn't been up-front with her from the start about his intentions. "I'm not looking for a buyer," she replied, pointing at the ground. "I'm staying put, right here on my twenty acres."

Adam shrugged, hiding his annoyance. "In

that case let's get these posies planted. I've got *cows* that need tending."

As they worked side by side in the dirt, silent except for an occasional comment or question about the placement of the plants, Emily felt her annoyance begin to fade. Perhaps it was only natural for the rugged rancher, no doubt steeped in traditional values, to take the man's side and assume she'd brought David out here against Stuart's wishes. Under the circumstances, wouldn't *any* normal father object to the move, or would he be able to put his son's safety above his own selfish feelings?

She could hardly blame Adam for Stuart's shortcomings.

"I'm sorry I snapped at you earlier," she mumbled, watching Adam poke a row of holes along one edge of the vegetable garden and stick a pansy in each depression. Emily went along behind him, surrounding each plant with dirt and patting it down. The sun warmed her back as she worked and the breeze tickled her neck. The weather here, she was discovering, was unpredictable, the temperature jumping and plunging from one day to the next like an unbroken horse.

Adam sat back on his heels and studied her from beneath the brim of his hat. "I had no right to make assumptions," he conceded after a long pause, surprising her. Stuart never admitted being wrong. "I imagine it takes courage to uproot yourself from what's familiar and start over somewhere new."

The unexpected compliment nearly unnerved her. "Thank you for that, but I don't know if it was courage or just desperation. Being dumped for a younger woman wasn't easy." Now why had she let that slip out? And what was it that flared in his green eyes before he blinked it away, a flash of sympathy? The last thing she wanted from her attractive, exasperating neighbor was pity.

"Your ex is nuts," he said bluntly. As Emily gaped, he ducked his head and popped another pansy from its plastic container. Faint color stained his cheekbones as he stabbed the trowel into the soft dirt.

An awkward silence stretched between them while Emily debated whether she should thank him yet again.

"Have you always lived here?" she asked instead. He certainly dressed the part of a cowboy bred to the bone, but she'd bet there was more to him than what showed on the surface.

"My old man was the one who started the ranch," he replied after a brief hesitation. "Although we've grown it a bit since he passed on." He glanced up, his narrowed gaze slicing across the horizon while Emily admired the strength of his profile. His incredibly thick lashes screened the expression in his eyes. "Except for being away at school, I've never lived anywhere else."

"Boarding school?" she asked, surprised.

"In a manner of speaking. University of Colorado." His tone was dry, as though he'd guessed the possibility of his attending college hadn't occurred to her.

"Oh." What a snob she was! "I met your brother and sister-in-law at church," she blurted to cover her faux pas.

His expression turned speculative. "That so? I haven't seen Rory except to wave this week, and I guess my brother didn't think to mention it."

"It probably slipped his mind," Emily replied, hoping she hadn't spoken out of turn. "They're a lovely little family, aren't they? And Rory was kind enough to introduce me to quite a few members of the congregation. Two of them paid me a visit the next day, Mrs. Price and Mrs. MacAffee."

Adam nodded. "People around here are friendly enough," he agreed. "But ten years from now you'll still be that newcomer from the coast."

"So you accept that I might still be here in ten years?" Emily couldn't resist asking.

Annoyance tightened his face, drawing attention to the shape of his mouth. The upper lip had a little dip in the middle and the corners seemed to tilt up or down with his mood, as though real smiles were costly or maybe just not worth the effort. "I don't have a crystal ball," he said shortly, dusting off his hands and straightening so that he towered over her. "Where do you want the tomato plants I brought?"

He allowed a person to get just so close, and then the wall went up, she thought. There was more she would have liked to ask, like whether he'd had fun shopping with his daughter and how the two of them got along, but Emily resisted, working mostly in silence. Meanwhile the sun's heat grew more intense.

"Would you like to take a break, have some lemonade?" she offered after they'd unloaded the last of the flats from the bed of his truck and set them around where she wanted them planted. He might be used to the abrupt changes in temperature, but her mouth was dry as dust.

He removed his hat and wiped his forehead

with a blue bandanna he then stuffed back into the pocket of his checkered shirt. "If it wouldn't be too much trouble."

"No trouble. I made it yesterday." She hesitated. "You can come inside if you want."

He glanced down at his boots, caked with dirt. "Thanks just the same, but I'd better wait out here."

The idea of him in her house made her feel vulnerable, so his refusal left her oddly relieved. "Okay. I'll just be a minute." She could feel his gaze on her as she crossed the yard. Was he remembering how she'd bolted up the same steps the other day? She must have looked like a silly greenhorn, afraid of being chased by a cow.

In moments she was back, carrying two sweating glasses filled with lemonade and tinkling ice. Silently she handed one to Adam. Inside the house she'd resisted the chance for quick primping, had refused to even glance in the mirror as she went by.

Thanking her politely, he downed half his lemonade in one long, thirsty swallow. Fascinated, Emily watched the muscles of his tanned throat ripple. Awareness of him as a man had her gulping from her own glass and then choking when the liquid went down the wrong way.

Adam took the glass from her hand before it could spill. "You okay?" he asked when she was done coughing.

Her eyes were watering and her nose was probably red. Lovely. "I'm fine," she croaked.

He returned her lemonade, and she took a cautious sip. "It's real good," he said.

"I made it from scratch," she admitted, as though he cared whether she'd squeezed lemons or mixed yellow powder.

"I could tell." The corners of his mouth lifted briefly. Pleasure way out of proportion to his comment washed through her. Oblivious to her reaction, he glanced around. "What do you do in the shed?" he asked. "You were coming out when I drove up, and it looks as though it's been fixed up."

"I've turned it into my studio," she replied.

His brows went up and he glanced at her hands. "You're an artist, then?"

Emily chuckled lightly. "In a manner of speaking. I restore books. Very old, very rare books." She took another swallow of lemonade and waited for his reaction. Why should it matter if he appreciated what she did, or even understood it?

"Huh," he said. "So I guess you're not looking for a job in these parts."

Was that disappointment in his voice? Had

he hoped her staying depended on finding employment? Would he perhaps even have used his influence to persuade people not to hire her?

She was getting paranoid. Besides, the question was moot. She had more work than she could handle.

"I'm lucky that I can set up shop just about anywhere," she replied, debating whether to offer a quick tour and then deciding it would reveal more of herself than she wanted just now.

Perversely she was annoyed that he didn't ask for one. Instead he handed back his empty glass. "Let's finish up, okay? The vet's coming by my place, and I want to catch him before he leaves."

When they were done, the garden and the flower beds looked nicer than they had before his cattle had trampled them. Conscience made Emily admit as much.

"They'll need watering," was his only reply as he bent to pat Monty's head.

Adam was in a hurry to leave. Spending time with her had been a mistake, one that left him of two minds whether he really wanted her gone. On the one hand, he needed her land; on the other, he felt a tug of attraction he'd have enjoyed exploring a little further if the situation had been different.

"That was a beautiful horse you were riding the other day," she said after he'd gathered up his tools and gloves.

She'd hit on one of his weak spots, talking about his beloved Appaloosas. "Thanks," he replied as she walked him to his truck. He tossed the shovel, rake and trowel into the back. "I've only been raising them for a few years now, but we're getting some good results."

"You breed horses as well as the cattle?" She looked surprised.

"It's a big ranch. Running cattle pays the bills, and we've always bred horses for the string. So far the Appies are just a sideline, but someday I'd like to change that." His father would be spinning in his grave at the idea, but the price of beef made diversifying a practical consideration. "Come by and see the foals sometime." He could have bitten out his tongue. What was he thinking?

"Actually, I'm in the market for a couple of mounts," she replied, her eyes bright with excitement. "Are any of your regular horses for sale?"

He couldn't resist. Scratching his chin, he

drawled, "As opposed to something irregular with, say, three legs or one big eye?"

Her grin snagged his breath. "As opposed to some high-priced, high-strung show horse with a pedigree I don't need," she said. "All I'm looking for is a couple of reliable rides."

He should tell her he was fresh out. He meant to, but the words didn't come. "We've got several that would do, a couple with spots here and there or some *regular* brown horses," he admitted instead.

"Perhaps my son and I could look at them sometime," she said cautiously.

Hell, he was in the business of selling horses. When she moved on, he could always buy them back and, if he was smart, make money on both ends of the deal. "Anytime." He opened the door of his truck and climbed in before his runaway mouth could get him into any more trouble. "You know the way?"

"I've gone by the entrance," she admitted. "It's pretty impressive." Color bloomed in her cheeks, drawing his attention to the fine texture of her skin. "I wasn't out looking for your place," she tacked on hastily. "I was just driving around and I went right past it."

He found her need to explain rather interesting. "I understand." He nodded gravely. "If you call first, I'll make sure there's someone available to show you the stock." It didn't have to be him, although he would like to see her sit a horse, thighs spread, clever hands buried in its mane or wrapped around the reins. He cut off the thought before it could wander. "Phone number's in the book."

Her head bobbed in agreement. Her hands were tucked into her jeans' pockets. "Thanks for replacing my plants so quickly."

Deciding it was time for him to put some distance between them and remind himself yet again just what it was he wanted from her, he turned the key in the ignition and touched his fingers to the brim of his hat. A moment later when he glanced in his rearview mirror, she'd already turned away, her trim hips swaying gently as she walked toward her house.

"Aren't Appaloosas the ones that are covered with spots, like those dogs from that kids' movie?" David asked as Emily drove down the road toward their neighbor's ranch.

She glanced at him sharply to see if his question had been derogatory. Although he drummed the fingers of one hand on his bent knee, his expression was merely curious. When she'd invited him to come with her, he'd done his best to maintain an air of studied indifference. Despite his attitude, she hoped the possibility of a horse of his own would snag his interest. Perhaps, too, it would give him something in common with the local kids.

"You mean Dalmatians," she replied as she slowed to turn from the main road onto Winchester land. "And I'm not sure if Appaloosas all have spots, but I guess we'll find out pretty soon."

She drove over the cattle guard and proceeded slowly past a boxy two-story house that had recently been painted light blue and trimmed in white. Pots of spring blooms on the deep porch, overflowing window boxes and lacy curtains all signaled a woman's touch. In the empty backyard, surrounded by a white picket fence, was a small swing set. It wasn't a house she could picture Adam living in.

"Looks like a pretty big place." David craned his neck as Emily noticed a larger, more modern house sitting on a rise of land surrounded by trees. Below the house was the turn Adam had told her to take to the stables. Straight ahead were numerous other buildings, making Emily realize what a huge operation the ranch must be. How many other, smaller spreads had already been gobbled up to feed Winchester greed?

"Well, from what I understand, there are three grown brothers," she replied as they passed the driveway to the bigger house. One wall was made of river rock and another mostly glass. No flower beds or frilly curtains softened the elegant design. No wide front porch framed the imposing double doors. No child's toys blocked access to the three-car garage.

"Remember that I told you I met the middle brother, Travis, and his family at church when you were sick," she added. "He and his wife have two kids, and they're expecting a third." Emily hadn't felt well herself last Sunday, so they had both missed the service. "You've met Adam. I'll bet this is his house."

David didn't reply, his attention on the long, low building ahead of them. It looked much newer than the other structures they'd seen, and it was surrounded by wood fencing. In the corrals were several horses. A mounted ranch hand rode by Emily's truck, touching his fingers to the brim of his hat when she caught his eye.

"This place is crawling with cowboys," David muttered under his breath.

"Behave," she admonished him mildly as

she pulled up next to a dusty Jeep. Adam's
pickup was parked by the open stable door.
The message she'd left with his housekeeper
had been answered by one he'd left on Emily's
machine while she was in town. She hadn't
spoken to him directly since he'd planted her
flowers, and she hadn't allowed herself to
wonder if she'd see him today.

A brown horse whinnied and a bay in another corral answered. As Emily got out of
her truck, the sounds and smells and dust reminded her a little of the riding stable back in
California, but this was clearly part of a working ranch. The fencing was unpainted, the
wood weathered to silver. An old horse trailer,
its paint faded and scratched, was parked next
to a newer, bigger model with the ranch's logo
in gold on the side. Across the road was a
smaller stable and a large round corral with
bleachers on one side.

"Which way do we go?" David asked as he
looked around, shifting impatiently from one
foot to the other, hands jammed in his pockets. "Do you think all those horses are for
sale?" He jerked his head toward the animals
that had come to the fence and were watching them curiously.

"I'm not sure." As Emily hesitated, she
heard the muffled sound of hoof beats fol-

lowed by a man's low voice. A moment later Adam appeared in the doorway of the second building leading a horse whose coat did indeed remind her of an oversize firehouse dog.

When Adam looked up, he hesitated slightly and then he brought the horse over to them. "You came," he said by way of a greeting, his glance flicking to David before it settled on Emily, his expression unreadable. He was dressed in his usual attire, right down to the worn jeans and leather gloves. Emily wore jeans, too, and Western boots, but David had insisted on baggy pants and tennis shoes with a brightly colored Hawaiian shirt.

"I got your message," she told Adam, ignoring her reaction to his rugged appearance as her hand tightened on her shoulder bag. "I appreciate your getting back to me so quickly."

"No problem." His expression thawed slightly. "I'm here to sell horses. Tell me what you're looking for and your levels of experience, and I'll show you what we have."

Briefly Emily described her riding background. When Adam glanced at David, who remained silent, she jumped into the awkward pause. "My son is a competent rider, too. I taught him myself. We'd like two reliable mounts to start with. Maybe I'll add more later, since I have plenty of room."

His eyebrows rose, and she braced herself for another comment about her land. "I have a nice Appaloosa mare and a couple of geldings, any of which would probably suit your needs, as well as a few other animals you could look at," was all he said. The horse with him tossed its head, making its spiky mane ripple, and blew out a long breath.

"What a beautiful creature," Emily exclaimed. "He's not the same one you were riding the other day."

The horse lowered its head and gave Adam's shoulder a playful shove that made him stagger. "This is Sinbad," he said, patting its neck. "He's a stud and a spoiled brat."

"And full of himself, like a typical male," Emily replied without thinking. From the corner of her eye, she caught David's startled expression as Adam's face relaxed into a genuine grin.

"Let's just say he's good at what he does, and he knows his worth," he drawled. Sinbad bobbed his head in apparent agreement. "He was the first Appy foaled here, and he's proven himself many times over."

David looked away, frowning, and Emily

wondered if this talk of studs and breeding, however vague, made him uncomfortable.

"Can we look at the horses you mentioned?" she asked Adam.

"Sure thing."

Another man appeared around the corner of the building. "Pete, would you turn Sinbad out for me?" Adam asked him.

With a friendly smile at Emily, the ranch hand took the stallion's lead, clucking to him. The horse's hooves, Emily noticed, were black-and-white striped, and his tail was short and coarse.

"Do you know much about the breed?" Adam asked as he led them around the outside of the stable. He directed the question at David, who shrugged. Emily bit her tongue to keep from prompting him.

"Weren't they developed by an Indian tribe?" he asked finally, surprising her.

Adam nodded. "That's right, the Nez Percé were the first ones to raise them. Most of their horses ended up slaughtered by the cavalry, but enough were spared to keep the breed alive."

"Slaughtered?" Emily echoed, horrified. "Why would they do something that awful?"

"It's a long story." Adam stopped at a corral fence and rested one booted foot on the bottom rung. "Our government in its wisdom did it partly to punish the tribe for resisting being placed on a reservation and partly to impoverish them and crush their spirit. Not a shining moment in our American history."

"Gee, that's awful," David muttered as the two occupants of the corral looked up. Emily didn't know what to say. The idea of anything so beautiful being deliberately killed, even though it had happened a long time ago, made her stomach churn.

"A few members of the tribe have started breeding them again," Adam said. He reached out to rub one of the inquisitive noses poking over the fence rail. "This is Shyla. She's in foal to Sinbad. Either of the geldings would work for you, too." The mare was a pretty thing, shaded gray and black with a distinctive white rump. Her sides were slightly rounded. One of the geldings was similarly marked, and the other was white with brown spots.

Adam glanced down at Emily's boots. "If you'd like a test ride, I'll saddle any of them that interest you."

"Can we go into the corral?" she asked.

He reached around her to trip the latch on the gate, and she nearly shied away like a skittish filly before she managed to stop herself.

"Sure you can." His voice caressed her ear. "Feel free to look them over. All my horses are as tame as cats and come with a clean bill of health."

David didn't say much while Emily circled the corral, first on the mare and then one of the geldings, and he didn't want to try either of them himself. She should have realized he hadn't intended to ride when he came out of his room in his tennis shoes. Had he picked up on the tension between her and Adam? Had she done or said anything to make David think she was flirting with the rancher?

Disappointed by her son's lack of enthusiasm, she dismounted reluctantly, declining Adam's offer to show them more horses. It was hard to tell him they'd get back to him when she was half in love with the mare already and thinking how fun it would be to raise a foal.

"Sure thing," he replied, glancing at David and then back at her. If Adam felt as though his time had been wasted, he didn't let it show. "If either of you want to look at the horses again or ride them before you make up your mind, give us a call and someone will help you."

Emily would have liked to strike a deal on Shyla and the spotted gelding, whose name was Puzzle, right then, but her enthusiasm had been dampened by her son's attitude. Maybe she'd buy both horses anyway and ride Puzzle when Shyla's pregnancy advanced, but first she needed to find out whether David wanted to keep looking for a different horse. She wasn't ready to give up on her pretty picture of them riding together.

"Thank you for your time," she told Adam, silently reminding herself that she couldn't be the only potential customer who didn't end up buying. "I'll let you know what we decide."

As they drove away, David surprised her with a favorable comment about Puzzle. "He looked pretty cool," he said. "I guess I wouldn't mind having a horse of my own."

Emily resisted a dry comeback about his underwhelming enthusiasm. "Why didn't you try him out while we were there?" she asked instead. From the corner of her eye, she saw him shrug.

"Couldn't you just buy him and then I could practice riding at home first? Everyone around here has probably ridden since they were little kids."

Understanding dawned, and she realized he hadn't been indifferent but rather was afraid of making a fool of himself in front of their neighbor. "I'm sure that's not true of everyone in Elbert county. There are probably riders at all different skill levels, just like anywhere else."

"Yeah, whatever," he mumbled, sliding down in the seat until he was sitting on his tailbone.

"What if I bought Puzzle and then you didn't like him?" she asked.

"You could take him back."

Emily realized that she wasn't going to convince David of anything today. Perhaps she'd ask Adam what his return policy was. "I'll give it some thought," was all she said.

As they drove back by the two-story blue house, she saw Rory sitting on the front porch. Feeling guilty for not doing anything about the other woman's invitation to get together for coffee, Emily slowed the truck as Rory glanced up from the book she was reading.

"Who's that?" David asked, the masculine approval in his tone spoiled when his voice cracked.

"The woman I told you I met at church," Emily replied, stifling her grin.

Rory walked over to the truck with a friendly smile. Even wearing jeans and a loose top over her rounded stomach, her height and her apricot-colored hair made her look glamorous. After the two women had exchanged greetings, Emily introduced David. "This is Rory Winchester, Adam's sister-in-law."

Rory ducked and peered in the window. "Another uprooted city slicker," she said warmly as she stuck out her hand. "How's it going?"

"Okay, I guess." David's cheeks turned pink as he gave her hand a quick shake through the open window.

"So you've been to visit Adam?" Rory asked Emily, blue eyes bright with curiosity.

"Actually we've been looking at a couple of saddle horses," Emily corrected her gently.

The other woman's crestfallen expression would have been comical in other circumstances, but Emily's awareness of Adam as a man was no laughing matter, especially in front of her son.

"You couldn't do better than Adam's Appaloosas," Rory replied loyally. "Which ones did he show you?"

"We're considering buying Shyla and Puzzle," Emily said.

Rory nodded knowingly. "What I really wanted to ask was whether you'd be interested in joining my new club."

"Club?" Emily echoed, dismayed. She wasn't really a joiner. Before she could reply, Rory chuckled.

"Don't look so horrified. I was only kidding, though actually the two of us should start a city slickers support group. We could be the charter members."

"But you've been here five years," Emily exclaimed. "You're a genuine ranch wife now."

"Like I told you before, once a newcomer, always a newcomer." Rory bent down and peered at David again. "I didn't mean you," she said apologetically. "Kids adjust faster. It's us old folks who have trouble."

David snorted and picked at the fabric covering his knee. "Whatever."

Before Emily could comment on his rudeness, Rory touched her arm. "Come for coffee someday soon. I could use some adult company, some *feminine* adult company."

"I will, really," Emily promised. "I've just been busy."

Rory nodded. "I understand. You have my phone number?"

Emily replied that she did, and Rory stepped back from the window of the pickup. "Well, I'll let you go for now. Nice meeting you, David."

He sat up straighter, possibly to make up for his earlier unpleasantness. "You, too."

As they drove through the gates onto the main road, Emily promised herself that she would call Rory soon. She had a feeling that the two of them could be friends.

"Is that a grin I see?" Emily teased David after he had parked his motorbike in his usual spot and removed his helmet. She'd been taking advantage of the balmy temperature to do a little weeding around the porch when she'd heard the familiar whine of his bike coming down the drive. "What have you done with my son?"

"Very funny, Mom." Despite his tone, he returned her smile with one of his own. It was probably the first genuine one she'd seen since she'd introduced him to the little pregnant cat he'd agreed could only be named Penny for its round copper eyes.

Emily rocked back on her heels and continued to study him with a blend of curiosity, exasperation and love so fierce that it made her chest burn. The shaved sides of his hair, she noticed, were growing out. The top he'd bleached carrot orange would take a little longer. Since reaching adolescence, he'd altered his hair and manner of dress several times. Although Stuart had fumed as each new version of his son appeared, Emily felt it was a basically harmless search for identity. Tempted to ask if David was considering adapting the local cowboy style next, she prudently held her tongue.

"How was school?" she asked instead, just as she did every day he didn't blow past her and hole up in his lair like an antisocial bear.

To her surprise, his smile remained in place as he shrugged. "Okay, I guess." His dark eyes actually sparkled. It had to be a trick of the light.

What a huge change from his usual response. She knew better than to question him further. Perhaps he'd elaborate over dinner. She intended telling him then that she'd decided to buy the horses, if he still wanted Puzzle. One of the reasons she'd bought this place was to have room for animals. "I made a pot of split pea soup," she volunteered.

"And that corn bread with the cheese and olive slices?" he asked.

His enthusiasm over her cooking pleased her and she nodded. "Of course. And I baked cookies this morning, so, have a few for your snack, but don't spoil your appetite for later." She tugged on a dandelion. "Do you have homework?"

"Of course," he echoed, but without the usual sneer. "I've got a biology test tomorrow, so I'd better get started."

He bounded up the steps like a puppy, all oversize feet, loose joints and gangly limbs, as Emily pried another dandelion from its hold on the soil, humming under her breath as she did. Something was afoot. Perhaps he was finally making friends here, or at least he'd stopped hating Colorado in general and Waterloo in particular. She knew he spent time every evening e-mailing a couple of old buddies from his school back in L.A.

From inside the house she heard the refrigerator door slam, followed a few moments later by loud, throbbing music from David's room. The bass tones seemed to vibrate in her gut. How could he study with that noise blasting away at his brain cells? She considered asking him to turn it down, but then she looked around and chuckled. Who was it going to bother, the cat?

The tune Emily had been humming shifted and picked up the pace, as did her weeding. Things were about to get better; she could feel it in her bones.

She didn't hear the vehicle coming down the driveway. She was aware of its approach through the vibration in the ground under her knees. As she glanced up, the now-familiar black ranch truck pulled to a stop in a cloud of dust.

Now what? With mixed emotions, Emily got to her feet, brushed the dirt from her knees and removed her garden gloves.

She'd intended to call Adam this evening about the horses after she'd talked to David. Was her neighbor here to tell her he'd changed his mind about selling to her? Not if he was a businessman.

Adam was out of the cab almost before his truck had come to a complete stop, swinging down as efficiently as a rodeo steer wrestler. The brim of his hat only partially hid a frown so black that it rivaled the pickup's paint job.

He advanced on her with his lips moving, but Emily couldn't make out what he'd said over the music still pouring from the window. She glanced over her shoulder, realizing a shouted request that David turn down the CD player would be futile. With her hand cupped behind her ear so that Adam would know she couldn't hear him, she hurried over to where he'd stopped to glare at David's motorbike as though he'd like to shoot it full of lead.

Her heart began to thump in her chest. Before she could ask him what his problem was, the song ended abruptly.

Adam thrust out his jaw, his angry voice filling the sudden silence as he jabbed a finger toward the house and then back at his own wide chest. "Tell that boy of yours to stay the hell away from my daughter or he's going to be dealing with me!"

...with the door, his jaw clenched. "If...
filled the porch when ... came upon her. ...
...to ask the impossible. I didn't try to hide
from danger, of that I was... and ... the
hell away from their ... or I just simply...
didn't ... the ...

Chapter Six

Adam's angry words came as such a complete shock that it took Emily a moment to switch gears from reluctant attraction to a flutter of anxiety and then straight through to protective rage. How dare he come onto her land and start giving her orders about her son!

As abruptly as it had stopped, David's music began to blare again. A hard ball of anger formed in Emily's chest, and her fingers curled into fists at her sides as she faced Adam down, chin thrust out aggressively.

"What are you talking about?" she shouted over the cacophony of sound from the house. "I'm sure David doesn't even know your daughter." Adam's furious expression made her tremble, but she'd vowed never to be cowed by a man's temper again.

"Oh, he knows her, all right," Adam sneered, sending a glare toward the house. "He gave her a ride home on that rolling deathtrap today." He jabbed his finger at the motor scooter parked near the porch.

Was *that* why David had been in such a good mood, because he'd met a girl? Emily gaped at Adam. "Is that all? You're angry because he gave her a ride?" For a moment, she'd been afraid Adam was going to accuse David of doing something he shouldn't have.

"Is that *all?*" Adam echoed. "Kim could have been killed!"

Emily resisted the urge to point out that he was overreacting. It was plain to see that Adam Winchester was a very protective father, but parental authority didn't give him the right to come onto Emily's property and criticize her son.

"How old is your daughter?" she asked, struggling for a reasonable tone. Part of her wished David would turn down the music, but considering Adam's state of mind it would be better if she defused the situation before her son even realized they had a visitor.

"Kim's fifteen and she isn't allowed to date."

Somehow that didn't surprise Emily. "Perhaps she didn't consider a lift home as a *date*," she replied. "I understand your concern, but I can assure you that David has his license and he's passed a safety course back in L.A. He's a very careful driver."

"Don't patronize me," Adam snapped. "I don't care if he drives like a little old lady. He's a menace, and I don't want Kim on that bike again."

Emily was beginning to feel sorry for the girl. Her father sounded like a first-rate tyrant. "It seems to me that you're telling the wrong person," she said sweetly as she folded her arms across her chest. "Shouldn't you be having this conversation with your daughter, or doesn't she leap to obey when you lay down the law?"

Dusky color ran up Adam's cheeks, and his eyes smoldered with impotent rage that nearly had Emily taking a step backward before she stopped herself.

His hand came up and she flinched, but he merely jabbed the air between them with his finger. "Don't concern yourself with my daughter. Just keep that boy of yours away from her."

Before Emily could sputter out a reply, he spun on his heel and stalked away, his back rigid. He climbed into his pickup and turned his head, their gazes clashing for a long moment. As she debated leaping up on the running board to continue their argument, he gunned the engine, swung the truck around and headed back down her road in a cloud of dust.

Emily nearly jumped up and down with frustration. All he'd had to do was to tell her nicely that he didn't want Kim riding the motorbike. How *dare* he suggest that David wasn't good enough to be friends with her! Adam's spaghetti-Western looks might speed up Emily's wayward pulse, but as far as she was concerned, his personality needed a transplant.

As Adam turned onto the main road, fighting for calm as he resisted the urge to floor the accelerator, his hands trembled on the steering wheel. How dare that woman question the way he raised his daughter! It was pretty damned obvious that she hadn't done such a hot job with that juvenile delinquent kid of hers, depriving him of his father's influence and then letting him run wild. Adam wouldn't be surprised to find out the kid had something to do with her leaving California. Maybe he'd gotten in some kind of trouble back there, which made him even more of a threat to a naive young girl like Kim. All the more reason for Adam to make damn sure Kim had nothing more to do with David.

Adam was still fuming when he pulled up in front of the showplace he'd built for Kim's mother, but at least he'd regained a measure of his control. He'd been working on the accounts earlier when he'd heard the bike pull up in front of the house, the sound of its engine as annoying as the whine of a mosquito. Curious, he'd glanced out his office window in time to see Kim dismount and hand back the helmet she'd just removed. Adam had recognized Emily's son by his ridiculous orange hair before he covered it with the same helmet, spun the bike around and roared away, his tires spitting dirt and gravel.

It had just been Kim's bad luck that Adam happened to be home in the middle of the afternoon. He'd met her at the front door, her explanation of missing the bus barely registering over the lurid images of motorcycle wrecks supplied by his imagination. He'd masked his fear with anger, ordering her to stay put until he got back and ignoring her tearful plea that he not humiliate her by confronting David.

Now when he walked back into the house,

he was greeted by an ominous silence. The moment he shut the door behind him, Betty appeared from the area of the kitchen, wiping her hands on her apron.

"Where have you been?" she asked. "You look fit to be tied."

Adam ignored her question as well as her expression of concern. "Where's my daughter?" he demanded through clenched teeth. It had occurred to him on the way home that today might not even be the first time Kim had ridden with that fool boy, but it was damn well going to be the last.

"She's in her room." If his housekeeper had intended to say anything more, his expression must have caused her to reconsider. With an audible sniff, she headed back down the hallway.

Adam dragged in a deep breath and trudged up the curving staircase. His anger was draining away, but the underlying fear for his baby's welfare still sloshed in his gut like cheap whiskey. He hated coming across as an ogre, but Kim was just too young to recognize the dangers lurking beyond the safety of her well-ordered world. As her father and her only accountable parent, it was Adam's responsibility to keep her safe from harm.

It was a duty he took very seriously.

* * *

After Adam's truck had disappeared down the road, Emily kicked at a stray pebble with her boot, muttering under her breath about overbearing, pigheaded ranchers before she finally went up the front steps with her head hanging. She hated having to tell David to keep his distance from the first friend he'd made since they came here.

Emily hadn't even noticed that the music had stopped again until she glanced up and saw him standing in the open doorway with his shoulder propped against the jamb. He wasn't the monster Adam had painted; he was only a boy—one who was growing up right before her eyes.

"Was Winchester here about the horses?" he asked.

In the face of Adam's rage, Emily had forgotten all about her earlier decision. "No," she admitted reluctantly as she joined her son on the porch, "that isn't why he came over." Touching his arm, she brushed past him into the house, wishing she could give him a hug and knowing he would probably stiffen if she did. Instead she sat on the couch and crossed her ankles primly. "Can we talk for a minute?"

"Sure." He collapsed into a chair opposite

her, his long legs sticking out in front of him. Something of her feelings must have shown on her face, because his own expression shifted from mere curiosity to guarded wariness. "Is this about me giving Kim a lift?"

"I'm afraid so."

David shot back to his feet. "What's the old man's problem?" His voice rose and cracked. He reminded Emily of a caged lion as he took a couple of restless steps and then spun back around to face her. "All I did was take her home after she missed the bus, I swear. She didn't want to call out there and have someone pick her up."

Emily was momentarily distracted by the idea of her attractive neighbor being described as an old man, but her attention quickly shifted back to David.

"Come on, honey, sit down," she coaxed. "Her father is just being protective. It's his right."

David glared at her, shoulders hunched. "So you're on his side?" he demanded with a sneer as he complied with her request.

"I'm not on anyone's side," she retorted, then bit her lip as she reconsidered. "No, of course that's not true. I'm on your side, sweetie, always. You know that. All I want to do is to find out what happened. I didn't realize you and Adam's daughter even knew each other."

"We got assigned to work on a class project together," David replied. "We were talking about it after school today, and we weren't paying attention to the time." He spread his hands. "It was no big deal. I loaned her my helmet."

Great, Emily thought. If they'd gotten hit by a car, her poor son might have suffered brain damage, but Princess Winchester would have been just fine.

Realizing she was being unfair, Emily studied her hands and tried to think what to say so David wouldn't take Adam's directive personally—even though *she* did. "Did Kim indicate in any way that her father might object to your giving her a ride?" she asked cautiously.

David shrugged and looked away. The guilty color flooding his face made her heart sink. "She might have mentioned that it would probably be okay because he'd be out herding cattle or something like that," he mumbled.

"Oh, David." Was she being selfish to think that now Adam had one *more* reason to resent their presence here?

"Kim's the only person in this dust bowl who's even bothered to be friendly!" David burst out. "Everyone else thinks I'm some kind of freak, just because I don't wear a cowboy hat and have straw sticking out of my a—ears." He slouched deeper into the chair, head bowed. "I don't suppose he'll sell us those horses now, either. Riding sounded sort of fun after I saw Puzzle."

Emily laughed ruefully. "Honey, this is Colorado. I'm sure someone else will sell us a couple of mounts." She sighed. "It might be a good idea if you limited your friendship with Kim just to school for now. No more rides on your bike, okay?"

He started to object, his chin thrust out.

"She's only fifteen," Emily continued quickly. "It might seem unfair, but her dad has the final say for a few more years."

"Yeah, whatever." David leaped to his feet. Why did he always seem to move at warp speed? "I've got homework," he said over his shoulder as he left the room with rapid strides.

After he had disappeared, shutting his bedroom door behind him with a solid thud, Emily replayed Adam's visit in her mind. Too bad he couldn't be bothered to look past her son's outward appearance. Perhaps if Emily talked to him again when he'd cooled off, explained that David was having a tough time with the transition and with making new friends, Adam would reconsider his stance.

If only she had an idea of what approach would work best with him. So far their encounters had been less than smooth. Even when they weren't actively disagreeing about something, there was an underlying tension between them that she hadn't been able to ignore.

Suddenly Emily had an idea. What better person to ask for advice about Adam than his sister-in-law, the woman who had apparently managed to figure out his brother? Surely the two men shared a few personality traits, even though Travis seemed far more approachable than his older sibling. Maybe Rory would be willing to give Emily some pointers.

Feeling slightly guilty for taking advantage of the redhead's outgoing nature, Emily retrieved her phone number from the kitchen drawer where she'd stashed it and picked up the receiver. It wasn't as though she was asking Rory to betray any family secrets. All she had to say was no.

"You treat me like a baby!" Kim burst out, flipping onto her stomach on her canopy bed and burying her face in her pillow. "You don't trust me!"

Adam stood in the doorway of her bedroom, the knot of fear and worry twisting his gut as his imagination supplied a vivid tableau of lurid motorcycle accidents. "It's not *you* that I don't trust," he argued, knowing it was futile. He'd just forbidden her to accept any more rides from Emily's son, and Kim had reacted exactly as he'd figured she would. If only she would trust him to know what was best for her.

He crossed to the bed and leaned over to touch her shoulder. "Baby, I just want to keep you safe."

She twisted away, turning to glare at him with swollen eyes. Her lips trembled. "No! You're just trying to keep me a prisoner, so I won't leave you like Mom did." As soon as the words were out, a look of horror crossed her tear-stained face, and she scrambled to her knees on the bed. "Daddy, I didn't mean that!"

The unfairness of Kim's accusation was a knife in Adam's heart. As an icy shroud of coldness engulfed him, he barely noticed the hand, fine-boned like Christie's, that his daughter extended. Did she really blame him for driving her mother away?

Had he expected too much from Christie, assuming she would adjust to life on the ranch and learn to love it as he did? Had there been more he could have done to make her stay? And what basic ingredient was missing in Adam that kept him from being the kind of husband—the kind of man—a woman wouldn't leave? First his mother and then his wife.

That was the crucial question, the one to which he still, after more than ten years, had no answer.

Would his daughter be the next one to abandon him?

Blindly Adam headed for the door, ignoring Kim's entreating voice. If Emily and her delinquent of a son hadn't moved in next door, he and his daughter wouldn't be arguing right now. The Johnson property would be part of the Running W as it was meant to be, their cattle would have plenty of water, and images of his sexy neighbor wouldn't be keeping Adam awake at night.

"Daddy?" Kim's voice had a quaver in it that tore at him, making him hesitate. "I'm sorry I said that. Are you okay?"

"Sure thing," he said gruffly with his hand on the doorknob. "Don't worry about it." He didn't turn to look at her, afraid her tear-drenched eyes would weaken his resolve about that damn boy and his bike. "I've got a business call to make before dinner. Just remember what I said. No more motorcycle rides."

As he headed back down the hallway, he glanced at the row of portraits displayed along one wall. From Kim's first birthday, he'd had her picture taken every year.

He stopped to study the fifth one in the row, when she'd entered kindergarten. On the first day of school he'd skipped a cattle auction to go with her. He wondered if she remembered how she'd clung to his hand. This year was the first time he hadn't driven her to school on opening day. She'd insisted on riding the bus instead.

He reached up to trace the curve of her cheek through the glass. He couldn't stop time from moving on, but neither was he ready to let her rush headlong into disaster. Not when he still had the ability to stop her.

"I need some pointers on how to handle Adam," Emily blurted, heat filling her cheeks the moment the words were out and she realized how they must sound to the woman seated across from her at the worn maple table.

When Emily had called Rory, she'd immediately extended an invitation for coffee. The way Rory had actually worded it was, *Please come and save what's left of my mind from the babble of small children.* Now, after a quick tour of the downstairs rooms, Rory had sent Steven and Lucy upstairs to play and led the way back to the kitchen, where she had served coffee and muffins with a graceful efficiency that belied her condition.

The two women had spent a few moments exchanging pleasantries before Emily blurted out her query about Adam. Now, as she saw Rory's eyes narrow with speculation, she realized how her question must have sounded.

"I didn't mean that quite the way it came out," she said.

Rory reached over to pat Emily's hand. "I like a woman who's direct, so don't be embarrassed about your interest in Adam."

"It's not that." Emily was almost stammering now, and her cheeks burned.

Stirring sugar into her coffee, Rory studied her. "You mean that you don't want advice about my attractive, single brother-in-law?"

"No, definitely not!" Some of Emily's horror at the idea must have been evident in her tone.

"You don't find him attractive?" Rory asked as Emily reached for a warm muffin.

For the space of a heartbeat, Emily considered bending the truth, but she disapproved of lies, even small white ones. Instead she shrugged. "When it comes to men, I've been vaccinated. I guess I'm just immune."

Rory laughed, as Emily had hoped she would. "Believe me, honey," she drawled, "I've had that shot, and its effects wear off after a while, so watch yourself. I denied my attraction to Travis at first, too." She sat back and patted her rounded stomach. "Just see where it got me."

"You look happy," Emily replied. "And you have a lovely family."

"Thank you." Rory's smile faded. "You know, when you and I met at church, I sensed that we could be friends. Just because Adam is my brother-in-law doesn't mean I'd ever repeat anything you told me in confidence." She sighed with obvious regret. "But you'd make such a cute couple."

Oh, dear. This wasn't going the way Emily had envisioned.

"I'm really not interested in him as a man," she insisted. That wasn't *entirely* true, but she was barely willing to admit it to herself. She wasn't about to confess to a Winchester, not even one as nice as Rory.

Rory pursed her lips, and Emily was afraid she'd taken offense. After all, Rory was married to Adam's brother. Although the two men were quite different in appearance, she supposed there was a family resemblance. It was obvious from Rory's condition that she found *her* Winchester husband attractive in the extreme.

"What a pity," Rory said lightly. "Adam needs someone in his life. He's way too focused on the ranch and on his daughter. Have you met Kim?"

"No, but my son has. He's a grade ahead of her at the high school." Maybe this would be easier than Emily had thought. She cleared her throat. "Actually, that's what I need advice about."

"I'm afraid teenagers are beyond me," Rory replied with a wave of her hand. "As you've noticed, my kids have a few years to go before they hit that entertaining stage." She broke off a piece of muffin and popped it into her mouth.

"Adam and David have gotten off on the wrong foot," Emily said bluntly. "I have to figure out a way to fix the situation between them, and that's why I need your advice."

Chapter Seven

If Rory was disappointed by Emily's revelation that she wanted advice for her son and not herself, it didn't show on the redhead's face. She sipped her coffee, studying Emily over the rim of her mug with arched brows.

"Why don't you tell me what happened," she invited.

Briefly Emily described her concern over David's adjustment at his new school, how he'd given Kim a ride home, even lending her his helmet, and her own subsequent confrontation with Adam.

"You've got quite a load on your plate, haven't you?" Rory noted sympathetically when Emily had finally run down. "I can certainly see why you're upset by my brother-in-law's ultimatum. Lord knows, when it comes to throwing his weight around, Adam is a pro."

"I wouldn't argue that," Emily replied dryly.

Rory glanced over at her nearly full coffee mug. "Would you like a warm-up?"

Emily shook her head. Maybe she'd said too much. "Thanks, but I'm just fine."

Rory nibbled on her full lower lip, obviously contemplating something. "You don't know much about Adam, do you?"

"Not really," Emily replied hesitantly. Where was this leading?

"Maybe if I let you in on a couple of things, you might understand why he's so overly protective when it comes to Kim."

What deep, dark secret was Rory about to reveal? Emily had secrets, too, and she wouldn't like the idea of someone sharing them without her knowledge or permission.

Abruptly she scooted back her chair.

"What's wrong?" Rory asked, eyes widening in obvious alarm.

"I'm sorry I took up your time with this." Emily got to her feet. "You're a Winchester and your loyalties belong with your family. Perhaps I'd better just go."

"Holy cow!" Rory exclaimed. "What is it

you think I'm going to tell you, that he murdered Kim's mother and buried her body behind the hay shed?"

Emily hesitated, one hand on her purse. "He didn't, did he?" she asked in an awkward attempt at lightness.

"Of course not. Now sit yourself back down." Rory's firm tone must have been the one she used on her children.

Emily sat.

"Give me a little credit," Rory continued, her gaze unwavering. "I'm not about to reveal anything that every soul in the county doesn't already know, okay? You'd know, too, if you weren't a newcomer."

"Okay," Emily replied, curiosity getting the better of her. "I'm listening."

Rory nodded her approval. "From what Travis has told me, Adam might darned near have been justified in doing away with Kim's mother, if she hadn't deserted him and Kim before he got the chance. Since Kim was just a baby, Adam's had to be both her father and mother."

"He has sole custody?" Emily asked. Although privately she suspected that Adam would be a difficult man to live with, she couldn't fathom a mother abandoning her child under any circumstances. If Stuart had fought for custody of their son, she didn't know what she would have done, but she was certain she wouldn't have left.

"Apparently Kim has never been a priority with Christie, which I, being a mother myself, cannot understand at all," Rory replied, flattening her hand over her heart. "To be fair, Adam did mention that lately the woman has made a few overtures, but now Kim's the one who's not interested."

"I can't blame the poor girl. Was the divorce a bitter one?" Emily asked, telling herself it was solely for her son's sake that she wanted to understand the man better.

Rory scrunched her nose, bringing attention to the freckles scattered over her fair skin. "I think part of the problem was that Adam's bride was a city girl who didn't have a clue about life on a working ranch. Not that I did, either, when I first came to Colorado, but that's another story. Adam's father died unexpectedly, giving him no choice but to quit college and come home. Travis and Charlie helped out, of course, but they were still in high school. The real responsibility of hanging on to the ranch fell squarely on Adam's shoulders. He worked around the clock. Poor Christie was stranded out here, miles from town, with a new baby and no help."

"It sounds as though life was no picnic for Adam, either," Emily exclaimed, incensed. "She should have been more understanding. He was only doing what he had to."

"Oh, I agree," Rory said. "They were both young, but he was obviously years beyond her in maturity. She did manage to stick it out through most of two winters, I'll give her that much, and I have to warn you if you don't already know, our winters are no picnic." Rory smoothed a hand down the shirt covering her gently protruding stomach. "Anyway, one evening Adam came in from a long, miserable day hauling feed to the cattle. I can just imagine that he was soaked through and cold to the bone. He found one of the men's wives taking care of the baby and a note from his loving wife. She'd had enough."

For a moment, Emily's heart surged with sympathy. Poor Adam! He must have been devastated.

"She'd gone to Denver," Rory continued. "Of course he dropped everything and went after her, but a couple days later he came back alone." She spread her hands wide. "As far as I know, he's never told anyone what took place when he confronted her, but he ended up with full custody of Kim. Travis suspects that Adam paid Christie off, because right after that he took out a personal loan at the bank. Then he worked a second job at the feed store for nearly two years to pay it off." Bending her head, she flicked a crumb from the tablecloth. "I probably shouldn't have told you that last part," she added quietly.

"I won't say anything to anyone," Emily assured her, "but how on earth did Adam ever cope with the ranch, a baby and another job? Was your mother-in-law here to help?"

Rory looked puzzled. "Oh, no. That's the really ironic part. When the boys were just young kids, their mother left. Adam's wife was the *second* woman in his life to abandon him. Now do you see why he's so overly protective of Kim? He's got to be afraid of losing her, too. As far as Adam knows, that's what the women in his life *do*. They leave."

"So his parents got a divorce, too?" Emily asked, picturing three confused little boys.

Rory shrugged. "The way I heard it was that one day they got home from school and their mom was gone. They've not heard from her since, not as much as a Christmas card. The sheriff investigated at the time, just to make sure nothing bad had happened to her, so he must have found some evidence that she was still alive. Travis told me their father wouldn't allow them to mention her at all after that, which must have been just awful for them."

Emily sat back in the chair and expelled the breath she'd been holding. "My God, that's terrible." How did anyone survive that kind of pain without breaking? She'd been grown and married when her parents were killed in a car accident. She'd been devastated, and their loss still affected her deeply, but could it compare to what Adam and his brothers had suffered?

"Poor Adam," she muttered. "And yet, doesn't he realize that what he fears most, losing his daughter, could very well happen if he smothers her? He certainly overreacted when David gave her a ride home, and I can only guess what Adam might have said to Kim."

Rory threw up her hands. "Travis and I, as well as Mrs. Clark, Adam's housekeeper, have all tried to make him see that. Unfortunately, when it comes to Kim, he's got a mental block." She smiled crookedly. "That said, do you want me to try talking to him about your son? I can't promise that he'll listen, but I could give it a try."

For just an instant Emily was tempted to grab Rory's offer, but when Emily had left Stuart, she'd vowed to stand on her own feet.

That meant fighting her own battles—even if they happened to involve her ruggedly attractive but less-than-approachable neighbor.

"Thank you for offering," she said reluctantly, "but I'd better talk to him myself."

"Is your son okay with that?" Rory asked.

Emily felt her cheeks go warm. David still hadn't entirely forgiven her for her *last* rescue attempt. "Who knows how he feels about anything?" she admitted ruefully. "The move has been difficult for him, and I have to do whatever I can to help him."

Rory's smile was gentle. "We all want to make things smoother for our children, and I don't expect that really changes much, no matter how big they get."

Emily thought of how she had uprooted David and dragged him with her to Colorado. "No," she agreed with a sigh. "That doesn't change." Then she remembered the way he'd tried to deal with his problem back in L.A. Handling Adam was definitely up to her, not her son.

"How old were Adam and his brothers when their mother left?" she asked, partly to change the subject, but also because she was curious.

"Oh, let's see. Travis was eight, so I guess

Adam must have been about eleven, and Charlie was just a little guy."

Emily remembered David at eleven, emulating his father as he struggled to be independent of her, an endearing little man-child who still needed his mother far more than he would have ever admitted. Her eyes blurred with sudden moisture.

"My heart aches for those little boys," she murmured as she blinked back tears of empathy.

"Most people tend to assume it was hardest on Charlie, because he was the baby," Rory mused, "but I disagree. Adam was the one who'd had his mother in his life the longest. Think how he must have felt to suddenly be without her. And from the little that Travis has let out, I gather their father was a stern disciplinarian."

"Did he abuse them?" Emily asked. She firmly believed that children needed love and understanding to help them adjust, not rigidity and rules. She and Stuart had never agreed on that.

Rory shrugged, the edges of her smile trembling just slightly. "Perhaps the old man, as they call him, was hard because he had a ranch to run, bitter because he'd lost his wife. To this day, if anyone dares to mention their mother, Travis really shuts down. He'll hardly discuss her with me."

"And Adam?" Emily asked, picturing a little boy with shaggy black hair and sad eyes. "How does he feel?"

"I've never had the nerve to ask him." The sound of footsteps on the stairs distracted Rory. "I believe my adult respite is nearly over," she said, getting heavily to her feet. "I was just about to check on the kids to see why they were so quiet."

Emily glanced at her watch. She still had work to do, and Rory had given her plenty to think about. "I'd better be going." She pushed back her chair as two little faces appeared in the doorway. "I've taken up enough of your time."

"I've enjoyed our visit." Rory gathered her children close and leaned down to peer at each of them. "And what mischief have you two been up to?"

Steven was twisting and giggling, trying to duck out from under her arm, but Lucy crowded against her, one thumb parked in her mouth as she stared shyly at Emily.

"We were playing trucks!" Steven exclaimed, adding some growling engine noises that made Emily smile in remembrance of David doing the same thing. At one point, being a long-haul trucker had been his life's ambition, right between firefighter and rock star.

"You have to promise to come back," Rory told her as they all headed toward the front door, Lucy still clinging shyly. "I've enjoyed our visit so much, and I do hope your son adjusts. The kids around here are really pretty nice."

Emily thanked her for the coffee and the advice, then bent down and said goodbye to the children.

"Do you have kids for me to play with?" Steven asked.

"My son is a teenager," she replied.

He looked disappointed, but Lucy removed her thumb long enough to whisper, "Bye."

Moments later, when Emily got into her truck, all three Winchesters waved from the porch. She felt a stab of emotion at the picture they made, and for a moment she envied Rory her family. As much as Emily valued her independence, she had always wanted more children.

As she drove slowly out the gate and headed home, she mulled over everything she'd learned about the man who alternately exasperated, attracted and infuriated her. If she had any sense at all, she would tell David to make some other new friends whose names didn't start with a *W,* and she'd do her best to avoid the rancher next door. Too bad Emily was already beginning to realize that ignoring Adam was far, far easier said than done.

Before she wrapped the Tuttle family Bible in protective packaging and placed it into a shipping carton with careful hands, Emily traced one finger over the gold lettering she had embossed on the dark-green goatskin cover, an exact duplicate of the badly worn original. The old book had once been a wedding gift from a bride to her new husband back in the 1830s, and Emily had just finished restoring it for the golden anniversary celebration of the grandparents of one of her first clients.

Restoration was intense, meticulous work done one careful step at a time, and drying glue could not be hurried, so she normally refused to set rigid deadlines. Back when she'd struggled to become established, Leslie Tuttle had sent other clients and lucrative commissions Emily's way. Against her better judgment, she had accepted this challenge only to discover that the damage to the family heirloom, by water and a glue-loving bookworm, was far more extensive than she had first thought. The foxing to remove the dark stains and the melding to repair the chewed pages took time, and she'd finished the project without one extra day to spare.

Before setting out for Waterloo with the irreplaceable cargo on the seat next to her and one eye on her watch, she called the express office in town to confirm their truck's departure time. She took a few precious minutes to check on Penny and nearly lost track of the time when she found the cat with four tiny kittens in a crate full of rags in the stable. Mother and babies seemed to be doing just fine, so Emily filled the cat's dishes and moved them into the empty stall that had just become a nursery.

Reluctantly, she left the little family, shut the stall door so that the old collie wouldn't upset Penny and headed for town. The morning was clear, and the road rolling out before her shimmered with the promise of unseasonable heat. Classical music poured from the upgraded stereo speakers, through the cab and out the open windows as she drove. At nearly the exact moment she remembered leaving her cell phone sitting on the dining room table, she noticed white smoke blowing up over the hood.

No, not smoke. Steam. A quick disbeliev-

ing glance at the gauges showed the temperature already climbing as the cooling system
lost its precious, vital water.

Swearing under her breath, Emily pulled
over to the shoulder of the road and killed
the engine. She looked both ways, but there
wasn't another car in sight. She turned on her
flashers, released the hood latch and hopped
out.

When it came to anything with four wheels
and an engine, she could check the fluids,
replace the wiper blades and once, in a real
pinch, she had managed to change a tire.
Anything more complicated was beyond her.
With a great deal of trepidation, she opened
the hood, leaping back with a squeak of fright
when the trapped steam boiled out. Either a
hose had ruptured, a clamp had broken or the
radiator itself had sprung a leak.

No matter what had caused the problem,
she'd have to abandon the truck for now and
hitch a lift to town. Emily cast a worried
glance at her watch, hoping someone would
come by soon. She'd ride on the back of a hay
wagon if it would get her to Waterloo before
the mail truck pulled out.

The warm sun beat down on her bare head,
and a headache nagged behind her sunglasses
as the minutes dragged by. She longed for her

phone and cursed her own stupidity. Staring at the flat, empty road until it began undulating like a belly dancer only made her eyes water. When she finally did see an approaching vehicle in the distance, her first thought was that she'd started to hallucinate.

Emily waited impatiently, squinting and straining her eyes behind the tinted lenses as the vehicle, another pickup, drew closer at a pace that seemed to rival that of a snail. Good thing this was rural Colorado and not L.A., or she would have been a lot more nervous about flagging down a stranger despite her desperation.

By the time the truck had pulled onto the dusty shoulder behind her, she realized that her would-be white knight was no stranger.

"Problems?" Adam asked after he sauntered over to where she waited. His eyes were shadowed by the brim of his hat, but one corner of his mouth was quirked into a near grin, as though he found her situation amusing.

Emily felt a rush of that same unwelcome attraction his appearance always stirred deep within her. "I think it's a broken hose," she replied briskly, "but don't let me hold you up. You must have important business in town." Surely someone else would appear at any moment—someone who didn't make her stomach flutter.

The faint curve to Adam's mouth flattened, and he hooked his thumbs into his wide leather belt, drawing her attention to the oval buckle and the very masculine fit of his jeans. They were faded, the denim so soft it did little to disguise his male contours.

"Oh, I'm in no hurry," he drawled as she redirected her gaze, "but unless you carry extra hoses and a water jug, you might be here a long time waiting for the cavalry to come along and rescue you."

"I don't need rescuing," she snapped, hackles rising. She'd been so preoccupied with getting this project done on time that she hadn't yet figured out a way to approach him about the situation with his daughter.

Her unfriendly response had stopped him in his tracks a half dozen feet from her. Perhaps he, too, was remembering their last clash. "So you'd rather take your chances than ride with me?" he asked in a neutral tone.

Wishing she could see his expression more clearly, Emily crossed her arms and stared down the empty road, biting her lip instead of responding. He'd acted like a jerk the last time she'd seen him, barging onto her property and venting his temper. Even his troubled past didn't give him the right to act like a knuckle-dragging Neanderthal, and she longed to tell him so. Between her lingering annoyance and her breathless susceptibility, she was reluctant to deal with him today.

After a moment of strained silence, he shrugged and swung away from her. "Suit yourself."

With a sigh of relief, Emily turned toward her truck. Through the open door she glimpsed the package she'd wrapped so carefully—the package that just had to reach San Diego on schedule. No matter what her own feelings might be, she couldn't possibly disappoint a client to whom she'd given her word.

It was plain Adam had only pulled over out of a sense of duty. She could accept a ride from him without mentioning their respective children. He probably had no more desire to discuss that situation than she did.

"Wait, please!" she called out, defeated.

His hand was already wrapped around the door handle of his black pickup, his foot on the running board. He merely looked back at her and waited expectantly.

"Um, could you give me a ride to town?" she asked, approaching him meekly. "I have to get to the express office before the truck leaves."

His brows rose. Did he have to act so damned arrogant? When he didn't reply, she figured he was going to refuse. She resisted a peek at her watch as perspiration trickled down the side of her cheek. Great. What was she going to do if he refused?

Finally he nodded, the movement uncharacteristically jerky. "Come on, then. We can send someone back to look at your truck."

Emily let out the breath she'd been holding. "Thank you."

Adam forced himself to stay where he was instead of rushing back to shut the hood while she gathered up her purse and a bulky package. Despite his foul mood, he nearly laughed when she rolled up her windows and carefully locked her doors. Where did she think she was, downtown L.A.?

She walked toward him along the shoulder of the empty road, her breasts bouncing gently under her lime-green T-shirt and her tan shorts exposing long, bare legs. He tried—with limited success—not to stare. Damn, but she was pretty, with her lips pursed in annoyance above the sexy cleft in her chin. Her cheeks were flushed, and he'd bet a prime steer that her eyes were shooting sparks behind her sunglasses.

He'd enjoy her annoyance more if he didn't

know he owed her some kind of apology for the way he'd yelled at her the other day. It was her kid he'd been mad at, not Emily.

He wanted to say something and get it out of the way, but the words stuck in his throat like a chicken bone, so he contented himself with walking around the truck to open her door.

It was obvious the gesture surprised her. Hadn't she figured a country bumpkin like him would have the rudiments of good manners?

"Thank you," she said again in that honey-sweet voice, scrambling into the high cab with her purse and package before he could extend a hand to help her, and affording him a view of her shapely rear in the snug shorts. She settled into the seat while he watched appreciatively and, when he didn't move, she glanced down at him with a puzzled frown. "I'd like to catch that delivery truck," she reminded him with a pointed glance at her watch.

It was his turn to flush. He shut her door with unnecessary force, circled back around and climbed behind the wheel.

"What time does it leave town?" he asked, starting the engine.

"In twenty minutes."

"No problem." He glanced into his side

mirror and pulled onto the empty road. He didn't look at her and she didn't speak again, but the vanilla scent she wore made blocking out her presence an impossibility.

He'd never been one to shirk his responsibility and he wasn't about to start now. "I'm sorry about the other day," he growled without taking his attention from the road. "I was out of line." He disliked apologies, either giving or getting, and he realized his hands were clenched on the wheel.

"I'm glad you've realized that you misjudged my son," Emily replied in a starched voice that reminded him of his last Sunday school teacher. "All he did was give your daughter a simple ride home. You overreacted."

Adam turned his head so fast he nearly snapped his neck. She was staring straight ahead, her hands folded neatly on the package in her lap.

"Whoa, lady, I never said I overreacted." Reluctantly he returned his attention to the road. It wasn't as though there was much traffic, but one never knew when a stray animal might wander through a break in the fence. "I was only apologizing for yelling at you, not for taking exception to your boy's risking my daughter's life."

"I'm sorry you see it that way." She sounded disappointed, but she surprised him by not adding anything else. She must be more concerned about getting to town than he'd thought. Did she think he was the kind of person who might order her out of his truck if she made him mad?

Adam felt like swearing under his breath, but he settled for clenching his jaw. He'd forbidden Kim to be friends with this woman's kid, so his own life would be a lot simpler if he could make the mother off-limits as well. Only trouble was, Adam's libido and his brain didn't seem to have even a nodding acquaintance these days.

"What have you got in the box, some kind of present?" he asked to break the uncomfortable silence.

"In a manner of speaking." Her voice thawed a degree or two. "It's an old Bible that's been in my client's family for nearly two centuries. She wanted it restored in time for her grandparents' anniversary party. That's why it has to go out today."

"What did you do to it?" he asked, more to make conversation than from any real interest.

As she described the damage the old book had suffered and the steps she'd taken to repair it, Adam found himself seduced by the passion in her voice and the graceful gestures of her hands. He was also intrigued by the idea of restoring something so old and fragile to its former condition, even though family history wasn't a subject that interested him, at least not his family's.

"I wish I could have seen it before and after you worked on it." He glanced at the package in her lap. "But how can you possibly duplicate the old lettering?" he asked. "There must be thousands of different type styles."

"I have drawers and drawers of fonts I've collected," she explained, "so in this case I was able to match the printing style on the damaged pages. Even the glue I use is the same formula." Her hands shifted restlessly in her lap. "I didn't mean to go on about it. My work must sound pretty boring to a man of action like you."

Her assumption that he must be too slow witted to appreciate her skill stung like a nettle. "You mean to a cowboy who probably hasn't cracked a book since he got out of school?" he drawled, offended, and then annoyed with himself for taking offense. Why should he care what she thought?

"Oh, good Lord, no!" The shock in her voice sounded genuine enough. To his surprise, she reached over to pat his bare hand as it rested on the wheel. For a moment her fingers lingered there, as light as a breath, and then she snatched them back. His skin tingled as though he'd brushed against an electric fence. The idea of turning down a dirt road and further exploring his reaction danced across his consciousness before he remembered, regretfully, the urgency of her errand.

That was why she'd accepted a ride from him, not because she'd welcome his interest.

Emily felt the casual contact of her hand on his all the way up her arm. She was glad her sunglasses hid her expression because she was sure her eyes must have widened in surprise. Her gesture had been automatic; she'd always been a toucher. From the tightening of Adam's mouth, he'd been put off by her familiarity.

She nearly apologized before she managed to bite back the words. Why call attention to her blunder?

"Are you always so paranoid about being put down?" she asked a little hotly, to cover her discomfiture. "Most people find book restoration as interesting as watching water evaporate. All I meant was that I didn't intend to ramble on about it in such excruciating detail. I certainly wasn't making an observation about either your IQ or your leisure-time activities, believe me."

Her words echoed in the silence while she wished she could take back the rash outburst. He was doing her a favor by giving her a lift and she sounded like an ungrateful witch. At least they were approaching the outskirts of Waterloo. She breathed a sigh of relief at the sight of scattered buildings up ahead.

"I guess I owe you another apology." He slowed down as they passed a row of small houses. "I seem to be racking them up today. Why don't you let me buy you lunch to show my remorse for misunderstanding your intentions."

His invitation caught her totally off guard. He couldn't possibly want to spend more time with her. "That's not necessary," she stammered, gripping the wrapped Bible tighter, as if doing so could hide the leap of reaction surging through her. "Besides, I, uh, need to see about my truck."

"No problem." He turned onto the main street through town. "After you deal with your package, we'll stop at the garage and leave Wally your keys. He's the local mechanic. Coincidentally he's also got the only tow truck in town. All I need to do is pick up some serum at the vet's. By the time we're done with lunch, Wally might have your truck fixed. If not, I'll give you a lift home."

"I hate to put you out," Emily protested. The idea of spending so much time in Adam's company was daunting. What if he realized that she was attracted to him, while he was only being neighborly? They had nothing in common except a couple of kids he was determined to keep separated. "You don't have time to deal with my problems."

He pulled into a parking spot in front of the express office, shifting to look her full in the face with his arm resting on the steering wheel.

"Lady, I'm the boss. I can make the time if I want." His voice was slightly rough, but his grin appeared genuine.

Being so close to him stopped her breath, and she would have given a good deal to know whether their proximity affected him in the least.

"I see," she managed. To her own ears, her voice sounded thin and slightly high. She couldn't look away. His eyes darkened as she studied him, and the pressure of her breath expanding in her chest made her dizzy.

An engine backfired, and Adam cleared his throat. "When does that express truck leave?" he prodded gently.

Emily blinked rapidly, remembering to breathe as she groped for the door handle. "I'd better go now," she babbled. "Thanks for the lift. I'm sure I can find Wally's on my own." She got the door open and all but fell from the cab, the precious Bible clamped against her breasts like a shield.

By the time she reached the wood sidewalk, heart thumping like a freeway blowout, Adam was beside her with her forgotten purse in his outstretched hand. "I'll wait for you," he said firmly as he gave it to her. "Go run your errand."

Like a scatterbrained child who'd been chided and dismissed, Emily fled into the express office, nearly mowing down an old man on his way out. He held the door wide and tipped his hat as she stuttered a mixture of thanks and apology.

After she'd filled out the appropriate forms for the insurance and shipment of her package, assured by the clerk that it should indeed arrive at its destination on schedule, she slipped the sunglasses down from the top of her head back onto her nose. As she went outside, part of her wished Adam would have decided she was far too strange to deal with and departed without her.

The other part, the feminine side she struggled to control in his presence with varying degrees of success, sighed with relief at the sight of him leaning against his pickup, talking on his cell phone. He glanced up and winked when he saw her.

"Wally can go out and get your truck right away," he said after he'd ended the conversation. "He's just leaving the café down the street, so we can give him the keys and then get some lunch. Have you eaten at Emma's before?"

"David and I had breakfast there once, I think." She remembered the homey old place where they'd stopped on their first day in town, with its faded curtains and wonderful smells, the curious stares of the other customers and David's sullen resentment.

His attitude had shown signs of change before Adam's ultimatum. Somehow Emily had to persuade Adam to ease up, but after what Rory had told her, was getting through to him even possible?

"Come on, then, let's go." Adam cupped her elbow lightly as he urged her back toward his truck. His fingers were warm on her bare, sensitized skin. Emily allowed him to open her door and give her a hand up, but all the while her practical side was blaring inside her head like an activated car alarm.

Was Adam the type of strong male every woman appreciated relying on in a pinch, or was he the same kind of overbearing, selfish jerk she'd finally managed to rid herself of after years of painful submission? And was she capable, even now, of knowing the difference?

Chapter Eight

Adam watched Emily study the menu selections. A frown pleated the skin between her feathery brows, making him want to reach over and smooth out the furrows with his thumb. He wanted—hell, when it came to the woman seated across from him, he wanted way too much. If only she had just sold him the damned land and left the county, his peace of mind would still be intact, and his daughter would be speaking to him.

At least after Emily had handed over her keys to Wally, who'd stammered like a kid when she gushed out her gratitude, she had removed her sunglasses so Adam didn't feel as if he was trying to assess her expression through tinted windows.

"What are you going to have?" he asked her as the waitress stopped by the booth, pencil and ticket pad poised expectantly.

Emily's head jerked up as though he'd taken a shot at her. "I'm sorry, what?"

Clearly her thoughts had been elsewhere. California, maybe? Was she pining for her ex and the life she'd left behind? "They make great burgers here," Adam pointed out mildly when she gave him a blank look.

"Mighty fine burgers," the waitress agreed. In her pink nylon uniform with its matching apron, hair net and sturdy rubber-soled shoes, Hazel Atherton had been a fixture at Emma's since she'd attended high school with Travis.

Relief washed over Emily's heart-shaped face, and she closed her menu. "That's what I'll have, a cheeseburger, with iced tea and lemon," she told Hazel decisively.

The waitress shot a sidelong glance at Adam, but she knew better than to say anything that might shrink the size of her tip. "Fries with that?" she asked Emily.

"No, thanks. A salad with ranch dressing on the side."

"Same for me," Adam said, "with the fries

instead of salad, bacon on the burger and coffee, black."

Hazel rolled her eyes. "I know how you take your coffee, Adam," she replied. Perhaps she figured he'd tip her no matter what, considering how they'd known each other for so long and that he was well aware she supported her elderly mother.

Once Hazel had walked away, he returned his attention to the woman sitting across from him.

"Small towns," she murmured. "No secrets, huh?"

Too damn true. Everyone in Waterloo knew the Winchester family history. They'd given their friends and neighbors plenty to chew on over the years, but he wasn't going to let the gossiping bother him, not today.

"Don't be concerned about that little toy truck of yours," he told her. "It's probably nothing serious."

"My truck's not a toy, and I'm not concerned," she replied with the feistiness he'd come to expect.

"Then what's bothering you?" He cocked his head to the side as he studied her and wished she'd left all that silky blond hair hanging loose around her face and neck today. "Are you worried about the Bible getting there on time?"

She shook her head, smiling her thanks when Hazel brought their beverages. "What makes you think anything's bothering me?" Emily retorted as she stirred sweetener into her tea. "My life's just fine. I have a son I'm proud of, a career that suits me and a new home I love."

Adam ignored the dig about her land. As the ice cubes clinked against her glass, he shrugged, unwilling to pry if it made her defensive. He had no right to grill her, after all. He'd only been making conversation.

"Have you thought any more about those Appies of mine that you looked at?" he asked instead, watching her wrap her lips around her straw. Reaction shot straight to his groin, and he took a hasty sip of his coffee, nearly burning his mouth.

"I didn't know if you'd still be willing to sell them to me," she said with a shrug, "but if you are, I'll take them both."

His feelings were mixed, but a sale was a sale. "Why would I have changed my mind?" he demanded.

Her eyelids fluttered. "We've agreed that our last meeting was less than cordial."

Heat of a different kind raced up his neck

and spread along his jaw. "I already admitted to overreacting," he muttered. Did she expect him to grovel for raising his voice?

Emily leaned forward, a smile softening her expression. "Does that mean you're willing to give my son another chance?"

Adam was vaguely aware of Hazel setting a plate in front of him. He felt crowded. Boxed in. First Kim and now Emily. What did she want from him? "I'll have to think about it," he replied.

Her smile faded as suddenly as it had appeared, leaving him with a vague sense of loss. "Fair enough, I guess."

He felt like a rat for letting her think there was a possibility he'd change his mind, but he wasn't about to debate the issue with Hazel hovering at his elbow. He glared up at the waitress.

"What?" he demanded, more sharply than he'd intended.

"Can I bring you anything else?" Her curiosity was obvious; her ears all but flapped. "Ketchup? Steak sauce?"

"Nothing," Adam snapped, painfully aware of the woman's weakness for gossip and wondering how much she'd already overheard or surmised.

In an hour the fact that he'd come into

the café with the new gal in town would be all over Waterloo like a hard frost. Well, it wouldn't be the first time tongues had wagged over the Winchesters. His mother's sudden departure had caused plenty of speculation, and his own divorce had stirred it all up again. He could hear it now: What was it about those boys and their women?

Rory's arrival in town as Charlie's mail-order bride and her subsequent marriage to Travis had only fed the fire, and anyone with most of their fingers knew the first baby had come early. As the ranch grew in size and prosperity, Adam had come to accept his family's greater prominence locally, but he still guarded his personal privacy, and Kim's, as best he could.

"You didn't need to bite her head off," Emily said with a disapproving expression after Hazel had departed with a toss of her head and a protesting squeak from her rubber-soled shoe.

Adam suspected that Emily was really referring more to the way he'd spoken to her than to the waitress. "Hazel and I go way back. I'll leave a big tip."

"So you're one of those men who think money can buy their way out of anything?" Emily demanded.

Adam gaped at her speechlessly. "Even if I did, which I don't, it wouldn't do me much good," he remarked when he'd recovered. "Ranchers' assets are on the hoof, not sitting in some bank. Bribing someone isn't usually an option unless they're interested in a good steak."

"I'm sorry." She ignored his weak joke. "I shouldn't have leaped to conclusions."

"Apology accepted," he replied. "We seem to be trading them today. Why don't you finish your lunch before it's stone cold." Filing away her bitter comment about men, he picked up the remainder of his own burger and bit into it. Someone must have let her down pretty badly, he realized as he watched her nibble at her bun. Was her ex-husband the culprit?

Emily piqued Adam's curiosity. Given his stand on their children, the last thing he needed was this edgy desire to figure her out. He should have his head examined. Hadn't Christie taught him anything about the staying power of city women?

"How's your sandwich?" he asked gruffly when he'd chewed and swallowed the bite that tasted like sawdust.

"It's very good, thank you," Emily replied politely. She set down her burger and began poking at her salad with her fork. "You're wrong about David," she added softly without looking up. "He's a good boy."

"Then why did you leave L.A. and separate him from his father?" Adam asked.

Her fork, a cherry tomato impaled on its tines, froze halfway to her mouth, and her expression turned haunted. "Because I was afraid if I didn't get my son away from there, someone was going to kill him."

The moment the words were out and Emily saw the shock on Adam's face, she wished she could take them back. Telling him about David's problems wasn't the best way to win Adam over. On the contrary, it might do just the opposite.

While she picked at her salad, Adam set his coffee mug down on the table without shifting his gaze from her face. Now that she'd opened Pandora's box, she could see that he wasn't going to let her shut it again.

"I beg your pardon," he said carefully. "Would you like to explain what you meant by that last remark?"

Emily swallowed the sudden lump in her throat. "It's not important." She had little hope of dissuading him. He was a father, after all, and she realized that she'd sent up a warning flare no responsible parent would ignore. Silently cursing her wayward tongue, she gave him the bare facts.

"Someone shot at David while he was out running one morning near our home. He claimed not to recognize them. Eventually the police decided it was just a random act of violence."

"He wasn't hurt?" Adam asked.

"No. Thank God they missed." She could still feel the fist of terror that had closed around her heart when he'd burst through the door to the kitchen, his face flushed from the exertion of running back to the house at full speed and his eyes still glazed with shock and fear. After the police arrived, her fear had been replaced at first by puzzlement and then frustration when David continued to maintain that he couldn't remember anything about the shooter or the car except its color—an unhelpful black.

She still might have accepted his story, however reluctantly, except for what had happened later. Now she blew out a breath, knowing Adam wouldn't let it drop until she told him the rest. He waited with a semblance of patience, but the big hands wrapped around his mug had gone white at the knuckles.

"And that's why you decided to leave L.A. and come out here to the middle of nowhere?"

he probed, like a surgeon looking for a hidden tumor.

"Not entirely," she admitted, surprised at his description of the area where he'd spent his life. "Of course I was worried, terrified actually, that whoever it was might try again. But David swore that he didn't have a clue as to any possible motive, and the cops were getting nowhere." She sucked in a breath, heart pounding at the memory of those days, of her sick fear, of Stuart's anger, of David's stonewalling. "He'd never been in trouble. He wasn't involved in drugs or gangs. We didn't know what to do." She swallowed. "Then one day the principal called. The school had gotten a tip and searched David's locker. They found a gun. Since they have a zero tolerance policy on firearms, of course he was expelled."

Adam's eyes narrowed. "A gun? Where'd he get it?"

She'd succeeded in surprising him, but the knowledge gave her no pleasure. "He'd stolen one of his father's pistols, along with some ammunition. Stuart, being the good father that he was, had taken David to the target range." She didn't even try to keep the edge of sarcasm from her voice, despite Adam's raised eyebrows. He probably took guns for granted, but she hated them.

"Once David finally realized the very real trouble he was in, he admitted to knowing who the other boys were, although he still wouldn't name them." Despite her repeated attempts to reason with him and his father's blustering threats, David had refused to budge. "All he would say was they were from another school. One of them apparently thought David had messed with his girlfriend."

"And did he?" Adam asked.

"He insisted that he barely knew the girl, and I believe him." She saw skepticism flash across Adam's face, but she ignored it. David might evade the truth on occasion, but she could usually tell when he was lying. "Of course, without his cooperation, the police were stymied. The detective did his best to assure me the whole problem would eventually blow over. That wasn't good enough for me, not with guns involved. David's father wanted to send him to boarding school back east. Instead I brought him here." She blew out a breath, aware that she hadn't helped her cause with Adam one bit. Now he would think the worst. "End of story."

He leaned back in his chair, his expression

unreadable. "That's quite a tale. And this is the boy you'd like me to approve as a friend for my daughter? A gun-toting hoodlum?"

"David is not a hoodlum!" Her sharp retort had several heads turning their way. Deliberately she dialed down the volume. "Toting pistols can't be all that unusual out here in the Wild West." Her lame attempt at humor fell flat. "We have no guns in the house," she said. "I won't allow them. It was a fluke, a one-time thing, because he was afraid for his life. He understands now that the way he handled it was totally inappropriate."

"Does he?" Adam asked.

She reached across the table and placed her hand on his, ignoring the heat of his skin. "Please, the adjustment has been difficult enough for him. He's been uprooted from everything he knows. A new school is always difficult. A new school in a new state—with everything so different from what he's known before—has to be even harder. So far your daughter seems to be his only friend."

"He sticks out like a peacock in a flock of crows," Adam retorted. "This isn't The Strip or Rodeo Drive, it's rural Colorado. He could try a little harder to fit in."

Emily knew that David's entire identity was still too tied up with his appearance for him to change it right away. It was one of the few things he could control when his life must be, to him, spinning *out* of control. "I'm hoping the horses, and riding, might help to bridge the gap," she said.

Adam shrugged. "You could get him into Little Britches. If he can ride decently, that might be a start."

"Little what?" she echoed, puzzled.

"It's a kind of rodeo club," he explained. "A lot of the local kids get together every week to compete." When Adam saw her dubious expression, he added, "It was just a thought. I can give you a name, if you're interested."

She was willing to grasp at anything. "Thanks, that would be great. Does Kim belong?"

He frowned. "As a matter of fact, she does."

"And are you going to give David another chance?" she pressed.

He glared at the French fries still on his plate. "Like I said, I'll have to think about it."

A few minutes later they left the café. It was too late for regrets, Emily told herself as she walked into the bright sunlight and slipped on her sunglasses. What was done was done. It wasn't her nature to hide things.

Maybe Adam would respect her honesty and find some compassion for her son.

While they'd been in the café with its lazy overhead fan moving the air, the temperature outside had heated up. Emily was darned glad she hadn't had to walk all the way to town or sit in her disabled truck for hours.

"That's Colorado," Adam replied when she remarked on the heat. "If you don't like the weather, wait a minute and it might change."

Once they were in his pickup with the windows open wide, he drove to the corner and turned down a side street. When he pulled in beside a long, low building with two big roll-up doors next to a sagging porch, Emily saw her truck parked around back.

Moments later she was relieved to learn from Wally that the problem, a broken hose, had already been fixed—and very reasonably, too, compared to L.A. rates. Had the mechanic given her a deal because he was under the impression that she was a friend of Adam's? She couldn't very well ask, not with the tall rancher hovering at her elbow while she paid the bill.

"Thank you for taking care of it so quickly," she said instead as she retrieved her keys.

"Yes, ma'am. Anytime." The mechanic's leathery cheeks turned pink as he touched grimy fingers to the bill of his cap, leaving a greasy smudge.

Back outside, Emily stopped, slipping on her sunglasses before she looked up at Adam.

"I'll walk you around to your truck," he said, touching her arm and then letting his hand drop back to his side.

Silently Emily followed him around the corner of the building. Except for several other vehicles, a battered Dumpster and a black dog dozing in the shade, the alley was deserted.

At the door of her pickup, she turned nervously to face him, glad her sunglasses hid her expression. Their earlier conversation had receded to a blur, leaving her attention focused sharply on the man who stirred her senses on a deeply feminine level.

"Thank you for the lift and lunch," she recited with her hands clasped tightly together as she struggled to block her awareness of him from her voice. "Now I've kept you from your errands long enough."

"Another minute isn't going to matter." Standing so close, he seemed even larger than before, more solid without being the least bit threatening—except to her peace of mind. She tried to step back, but her butt bumped the fender of her truck. There was no room to retreat. If she didn't get out of here, she was going to start batting her lashes and licking her lips.

He leaned closer with a frown on his face. Perhaps he was annoyed at the time she'd cost him, but he was the one to insist on lunch.

With one hand he removed her sunglasses, careful not to hook them on her ears, and set them on the hood of her truck. Emily's breath snagged in her throat as he cupped her chin lightly. He was near enough for her to see that the green of his irises was only a thin band around the black of his pupils.

"I'm going to be damned sorry I did this," he muttered, sounding annoyed as Emily stared up at him.

Perhaps she should have protested or pushed him away, but she was too caught up in his expression of hungry intent, like that of a predator focused totally on its prey. Since Emily was always honest with herself, brutally so, she knew, too, that she'd speculated way too much about the feel of that firm mouth and the taste of him to turn away now. She wasn't about to miss this chance to satisfy her curiosity.

He hesitated for a moment, and she realized he was giving her a chance to stop him. His grip on her chin was light enough for her to pull away easily, but she stood very still. What she wanted to do was to lean into him. When her lips parted in anticipation, he groaned low in his throat, a harsh sound, and then he bent his head.

I was right about regretting this, Adam thought as his lips touched hers. They were as soft and plump as satin pillows, but not nearly as passive as they shaped themselves to his mouth. When he dipped his tongue inside and sampled her sweetness, his brain faltered and all thought blurred. Pure feeling took over, crowding out everything else.

He was vaguely aware of her flattened palms resting against his chest, of his own hands wrapped around her upper arms, of a moan she could have made—or that might have come from him. He wanted to press her up against the door of her truck, or maybe lay her across the hood and crawl up there on top of her. Instead he peeled his mouth off hers, and it was like taking duct tape off cardboard. Not easy, not at all. But it had to be done before he just pushed her down in the dust of the alley and let pure lust take over.

Her eyes, when he could finally focus on them, fluttered open to stare blankly back at him.

"You okay?" His voice was hoarse.

She blinked and her eyes cleared, her cheeks turning the color of a painful sunburn. He thought about apologizing and decided not to. For this harebrained maneuver, he'd do his penance in sleepless nights instead.

"Yes, of course I'm okay." Her voice was an octave higher than usual and her lips curved in a welcome it was damned hard to ignore, but ignore it he did. Jamming his hat tighter onto his head, he managed something he hoped was articulate and turned away before he could succumb to temptation and sink into her again.

Emily watched his long strides take him back around the corner, she pressed the fingers of one hand to lips that still tingled. Now that her curiosity had been satisfied, she almost wished she could turn back the clock to before he'd kissed her.

Almost.

When Emily arrived back home, so preoccupied with what had happened in the alley behind Wally's Auto Repair that she was barely aware of the drive from town, she received another shock. She parked next to David's motorbike and got out of the truck, touching her tongue to her upper lip as though

Adam's kiss was still imprinted on her mouth for her impressionable son to see.

David came down the front steps to meet her as though he'd been listening for the sound of her truck. At his side was Monty, who waited patiently every day for David's return from school. At first she didn't notice anything unusual, probably because she was too busy hiding her own inner turmoil. As she got closer, she realized that something about David's appearance was different.

"What did you do to your hair?" she blurted out. It was darker and a whole lot shorter than it had been this morning when he left for school.

He rolled his shoulders forward and ducked his head self-consciously, his hands stuffed deep into the pockets of his baggy jeans as Emily bent to pat Monty's head. David's brassy orange locks were gone, exposing the natural brown roots that had been growing in.

"I got it cut in town." His tone was defiant as he met her gaze, but his expression revealed a vulnerability that tugged at her heart. The new style made him look younger and, she thought, much more handsome.

He ran the palm of one hand over his head. "It was time for a change."

"I like it." Emily wasn't sure whether he'd

take her stamp of approval as a reason to alter his appearance even more drastically the next time. When she and Stuart had told him they were splitting up, he'd dyed his hair bright green and gotten his ear pierced in four places. Now she realized he'd replaced the row of gold hoops with a single discreet stud. What was going on?

He stared down at his feet. "I wondered if we could buy me some new clothes?" he mumbled, surprising her even further. "For school and stuff."

Stuff? Emily was speechless. They'd argued so much over what he wore that she'd finally taken the coward's way out, giving him money so he could shop on his own. He'd bought his bizarre wardrobe at thrift shops and vintage clothing stores, but as long as he didn't wear anything truly offensive, she hadn't objected.

"What did you have in mind?" she asked carefully when she could find her voice.

Self-consciousness radiated from him in waves, and the last thing she wanted was to spook him. The happy dance she felt like performing would have to wait.

He lifted up one foot and pointed at the expensive, name-brand athletic shoe he'd wanted so badly and that Stuart had squawked about paying for.

"If we're getting horses, I'll need some boots," David said. He set his foot back down and bent to examine the length of his baggy pant legs. Seen from the top, his hair looked downright ordinary. "And maybe some regular jeans."

This new development was almost as startling to Emily as being kissed passionately by her neighbor. She was dying to ask her son what had brought about his reformation, but she knew better than to pry. He'd clam up, and he might even change his mind.

"Let's go to Denver in the morning," she suggested eagerly. The next day was Saturday and the big city was less than a two-hour drive. She could pick up a few things for herself while they were there, they'd have lunch and maybe visit the museum.

"Uh, that's okay," he said, wrinkling his nose. "Somebody at school sort of mentioned a store in town that might have what I need. Can we just look there first?"

Emily bobbed her head, disappointment and surprise mingling together. David shopping for clothes in Waterloo with—his words—the hicks and the hayseeds? She had to remind herself that she could go to Denver anytime. This giant step her son was taking and her hopes that it would help him to fit in were more important than sight-seeing or fine-tuning her own wardrobe.

"Sure thing," she replied. "We'll go in the morning. I'll start dinner in a few minutes, but first I need to check on Penny. Want to come with me?"

David's brow wrinkled in puzzlement, but he must have seen the sparkle of excitement in her eyes, because his frown cleared abruptly. "Did she have her kittens?" he asked.

"She sure did." Emily was eager to see how they'd changed in the last few hours. "I found them in a stall this morning before I left for town."

"How many did she have?" he asked as they walked together toward the stable with the dog following along behind them.

Emily found herself grinning at David's enthusiasm. "Come on and see for yourself."

She'd been worried that they might run into Adam while they were in Waterloo, but she hadn't seen his familiar black pickup parked on the main street as she drove David to the Western Wear store with the false front and the sign outlined in thick rope. After she followed David inside, he grabbed several pair of jeans, checked the sizes and disappeared into a fitting room. While Emily looked at brightly colored women's shirts jammed together on a circular rack on the other side of the crowded shop, she kept darting nervous glances over her shoulder at the front door.

She wasn't ready to face Adam yet, and she had no idea how she would act when she saw him next. Had the kiss been an impulse on his part? Had it meant anything to him, or was it just an experiment? She was still trying to figure out why his feelings about the incident even *mattered* to her. Half the time he made her spitting mad and the other half he intrigued the heck out of her. Neither reaction made her comfortable.

When David came out wearing new dark-blue jeans, she was happy to pay for them, another pair that looked identical and a leather belt with a plain brass buckle. After the clerk put them and his old pants into a sack, David led Emily next door where they were both fitted for riding boots. He wanted plain brown with squared-off toes, but Emily treated herself to a navy blue pair with ornate stitching on the sides. After she tucked her credit card back into her wallet, he picked up both big boxes and she carried the bag with his clothes.

"Do you want to stop for lunch?" she asked, turning back to him as they reached the front door of the bootery.

To her surprise, he shook his head. "Naw, I'm not hungry. Could we just go home? You probably want to check on the kittens, anyway."

Emily was relieved by his suggestion. As proud as she was of his altered appearance, she didn't really want to subject either of them to the curious stares of the café patrons today, nor to chance running into Adam before she'd figured out how to deal with him. Even so, David's apparent lack of appetite brought with it a jab of maternal concern.

"I think you're the one who wants to see the kittens," she teased. Since his last growth spurt, she had to tip back her head to look at him, and now his altered appearance was still a pleasant surprise each time she did.

He shifted their bulky purchases from one arm to the other. "They're pretty cool."

She nearly chuckled at his admission. Last night he'd stayed in the stable watching them for an hour. "I'll fix us something to eat when we get home." She swung around and reached for the door just as it was pulled open from the outside. Caught off balance, she nearly collided with a pretty young girl coming through it.

Emily was about to excuse herself, but the girl's gaze darted past her as though she were invisible, the green eyes that seemed somehow familiar widening in surprise.

"David!" the girl exclaimed, her cheeks flushing with color. "You look so different! What are you doing here?"

Behind the teenager in the doorway, Adam's gaze locked with Emily's, and she realized belatedly that the pretty young thing smiling adoringly up at her son was Winchester's off-limits daughter, Kim.

Chapter Nine

Adam caught a glimpse of Emily's startled face and then he bumped into Kim, who'd stopped in the open doorway. His hand shot out automatically to grab her shoulder and steady her.

His daughter shrugged away from his touch, a not-so-subtle reminder that she was still ticked off by his refusal to let her run wild. Eventually she'd realize he was only trying to protect her. Meanwhile she needed new riding boots, and she had no problem with his money, just him, so here they were—face-to-face with the woman he'd like nothing better than to *drive* wild.

Emily's cheeks had gone as pink as a desert sunrise, and her lips—whose touch and texture he hadn't been able to get out of his head since he'd complicated his life by tasting them—were parted in obvious surprise. Standing beside her was that son of hers.

At least Adam assumed it was the same kid, although he looked so ordinary that Adam wouldn't have recognized him if Kim hadn't greeted him by name.

For a moment the four of them stood awkwardly, their gazes darting around so quickly they could have been watching a goat-tying competition played at fast-forward.

"Adam! Kim, dear, how are you?" asked the proprietor of the boot shop, a widow whose dinner invitations Adam had dodged on more than one occasion. So far his reluctance hadn't deterred Harriet Parks. Even now, as he tore his gaze from Emily's, Harriet was advancing on him with both hands outstretched like claws.

"Hello, Harriet," he replied, taking a step back. "How are you?" As usual, her makeup was overdone and her hair appeared to have been combed with a tumbleweed.

Her blue eyes, the same startling shade as her upper lids, narrowed. "Do you all know each other?" she cooed with the patently false smile of a salesperson evaluating her customers' financial worth. Whenever he was around Harriet, Adam always came away feeling as if he'd had his pockets picked.

He nodded at the same time that Emily shook her head, her gaze on Kim.

Wishing Harriet would disappear in a cloud of her too-intense perfume, he risked rejection by again touching Kim's shoulder. "Emily Major, my daughter, Kim," he said. "Honey, this is our new neighbor. You know her son."

Emily's smile nearly curled his toes inside his boots. Too bad its warmth wasn't aimed at him. "It's nice to meet you," Emily said, shifting to include her son. "David has mentioned you."

She slanted a warning glance at Adam, as though to keep him from blurting out anything inappropriate. If she knew what a sharp-tongued shrew Harriet could be, she wouldn't have worried. Some of Harriet's comments about Rory and Travis had gotten back to Adam. Blue eye shadow could be changed; a mean spirit was harder to fix.

"David and I are friends," Kim replied with a toss of her head and a sidewise look at Adam. "The project we did together got an A-minus."

Adam lifted an eyebrow. It was the first

he'd heard about that. David flushed, but didn't say anything. Emily rushed in to fill the awkward pause as the phone behind the counter began to ring. With a reluctant glance over her shoulder, Harriet muttered an apology and rushed off to answer it.

"You have biology together, don't you?" Emily asked Kim.

"World history," she corrected.

"How do you like it?"

Kim's gaze darted to David and then back to Emily's. "It's okay, but the teacher, Mr. Ambrose, is kind of a dork," she replied with another flip of her hair. "Don't you think so?" she prodded David.

"All teachers are dorks," he replied, shifting the two boxes he was carrying from one arm to the other.

"Oh, you got boots," Kim exclaimed. "Cool."

"Riding boots," Emily said. "I think your dad is going to sell us a couple of his horses." She looked at Adam with a slight frown. "I meant to call and see if you'd be willing to deliver them, since I haven't bought a trailer yet."

"Sure thing." And he'd make damn certain it was while her son was in school. Adam didn't need a chaperon while he tried to find out whether his attraction to this woman was returned. Just because she hadn't fought him off when he'd kissed her didn't necessarily mean much. "How about Monday, around noon?"

Emily's mouth compressed into an intriguing pout, and she clasped her hands together in front of her. "I know I should have contacted you sooner, but I was hoping you could bring them over this weekend while David's home to help me get them settled."

What could Adam say to that? "How about this afternoon, around three?"

"Thank you." Her smile made rearranging his schedule worthwhile, but he'd have to call the cattle broker on his cell phone and postpone their appointment.

Kim's gaze darted between Emily and her dad, her expression speculative. "Maybe I'd better come along and help you unload the horses."

Did that mean Adam was forgiven? "We'll see," he replied. Maybe it would be a good idea for him to observe her behavior around the boy. She was too damned young for a flirtation, despite the way she'd been acting since they walked into the boot shop.

Emily glanced over at Harriet, who was ending her phone call. "Well, I guess we'd better let you get on with your shopping. I need to stop at the co-op and pick up a few things." She smiled at Kim. "Kim, it was nice to meet you. I hope we'll see you again."

"Count on it," Kim replied, surprising Adam by hooking her arm through his. "My dad and I will be over later." She bade David goodbye and glanced at Adam expectantly.

Automatically he touched two fingers to his hat brim. "See you at three," he told Emily. Then he exchanged nods with David and followed his daughter deeper into Harriet's lair.

"So that was Kim," Emily said inanely as she backed her truck from its parking space and headed down the main street toward the feed store. Had David noticed the way Emily had blushed every time the girl's father looked at her? When Adam had first walked into the boot shop, could David have heard her heart start hammering in her chest like the drum in a heavy-metal band? Had her voice revealed her inner turmoil?

"Yeah, that's her." David slouched lower in his seat. "I guess her old man was pretty surprised when I didn't jump her right in front of him, huh?"

"David!" Emily sputtered. "She's his only child and she's fifteen years old. He's just a little overprotective, that's all."

David snorted. "Yeah, right. You can see that he hates my guts."

"He doesn't even know you," Emily argued. "I'm sure he'll change his attitude once he does." She parked in front of the old wooden building where she'd first—quite literally—bumped into Adam. "You're a great kid," she told David as she turned off the ignition and faced him. "You can let Adam see that when he brings the horses over, or you can give him attitude and prove him right. It's your choice."

For once her son's expression was impossible for her to read. "Nothing in my life is my choice," he muttered.

At a loss for what to say, Emily got out of the truck and went inside. David followed slowly. She hoped that Adam would realize David was making an effort to fit in. Emily had envied the way Kim had unselfconsciously linked arms with her dad back at the boot shop. It was obvious they were close. Emily hoped that she and David would regain their closeness and that Adam's horses would help it to happen.

After the supplies Emily had bought were loaded, she stopped at the local drive-in for burgers. There were several teenagers surrounding an old Ford pickup that had been newly painted. Emily wondered if David knew them, but he merely glanced out the window and then insisted on waiting for her in the truck.

When she came back out, one of the boys was talking to David through his open window.

"This is Matt," he said. "My mom."

Like Adam had done, the other boy touched the brim of his hat politely. "Ma'am."

Emily would have liked to chat for a few moments, but she knew how easy it was to mortify her teenager, so after a brief hello, she held up the bags of food. "We'd better go before this gets cold."

"See you at school," Matt told David. "Nice to meet you, ma'am."

"Emily!" she corrected him with a smile.

"Emily," he repeated. "Yes, ma'am."

"Let's eat at that little park," Emily suggested as she left the lot surrounding the drive-in.

David agreed. While they ate, she resisted the urge to quiz him about the other boy. "We'll have just enough time to get the stalls ready before Adam arrives," she said instead between bites of her hamburger. Maybe she'd even have a minute to run a brush through her hair and renew her lip gloss. Changing into a different shirt was out of the question. David would notice, and she had no idea how he would react if he thought she was interested in someone, even casually. His father's remarriage had been hard enough on him.

Not that *she* had any plans to marry again, not for a very long time if ever.

As David devoured his bacon burger, he merely grunted in reply to her statement, making Emily wonder if she'd been wrong in thinking he was looking forward to getting the horses delivered. In the bed of the pickup were several bales of hay and sacks of grain, a new wheelbarrow, assorted rakes and pitchforks, a shovel, a broom, some tack and a collection of grooming items. Over David's protests, she'd insisted on rubber boots for both of them. The bedding for the stalls had been delivered a couple of days before, and the stable was reasonably clean, thanks to their combined efforts. He'd only grumbled a little bit.

"If you'd unload the truck, I'll hang the hay nets and fill the water dispensers," she said. The tack room could be organized later. For now she was eager to get their new residents settled in.

To her relief, David's expression brightened. "Yeah, I can do that. How soon can we ride?"

"Tomorrow?" Emily suggested. "I'll ask Adam, but I expect they'll need the rest of today to adjust to the new surroundings."

"Can I call Dad and tell him about them?" David asked. "I want to talk to him about my visit this summer, too."

"Why don't you e-mail him instead," she suggested, swallowing a sigh of disappointment. "It's cheaper." And perhaps Stuart would actually reply this time, although he'd been evasive so far about David's vacation.

"Okay." As soon as Emily was done eating, she stuffed her wrappers back into the bag and headed for home. David turned on the stereo, but when a piano concerto poured from the speakers, he quickly changed the station. Then he finished his milk shake with a last noisy slurp that Emily ignored.

As they passed the spot where Adam had picked her up the other morning, his rugged image filled her mind. She would have to fight her attraction to him if she was to maintain her hard-won independence, but it wasn't going to be easy.

Beside her, David began picking at his fingernail. "Mom?"

"What is it?" She turned onto their road,

possessive pride swelling in her chest like a helium balloon as she looked at the cluster of buildings. All theirs. My, but it felt good.

"Do we have enough money?"

Her head snapped around, and her mouth fell open. "Why do you ask?"

He squirmed in his seat. "I just wondered. Is Dad like, paying you what he's supposed to? For me, I mean?" His voice squeaked, and he cleared his throat. "I know he's got a lot of other expenses right now."

Emily slowed the truck and backed it around close to the stable. Touched by her son's concern, she reached over to pat his arm. "I make a good living. The money your father sends goes right into your college fund, so don't worry, okay? We're fine."

"Really?" he asked, frowning.

"Really."

After a moment, his expression cleared. "Okay. So if Dad can't afford my plane ticket this summer, you'll buy it?"

Stuart was supposed to pay for David's airfare to L.A. and back. As much as Emily disliked the idea of her son's return to California, he missed his father. She wasn't about to let her own concerns or Stuart's flimsy excuses stand in the way of David's happiness.

"We'll work something out," she promised,

wondering what Stuart had been telling him. The man made an excellent living, but she imagined that his new trophy wife was an expensive commodity.

Looking relieved, David opened his door and unfolded his lanky frame. Before Emily had managed to grab her purse and keys and fumble open her own door, he already had the tailgate lowered and a sack of feed propped onto his shoulder.

"Be careful you don't hurt yourself." The words popped from Emily's mouth before she had a chance to bite them back, but he only rolled his eyes and grinned as he headed for the stable.

For the next hour they worked in mostly silent compatibility. Emily checked on Penny several times to make sure all the activity wasn't alarming the cat, but she seemed content.

After the stalls were done, Emily was just about to duck into the house for a minute when she heard the low rumble of Adam's pickup.

"They're here," David said unnecessarily.

She wondered how much of his enthusiasm had to do with seeing Kim again. She was a pretty girl, with long, dark hair and a slim but promising figure. Her mother must have been a beauty.

Emily felt a spurt of jealousy, quickly suppressed, and then she joined her son at the edge of the driveway. His stance was deliberately casual, but she could see the tension in his shoulders. She would have sworn they'd broadened beneath his T-shirt since the last time she'd noticed.

Adam was pulling a small horse trailer, but he sat alone in the cab.

"Where's your daughter?" Emily asked after he'd turned off the noisy diesel engine and climbed down. She figured David would be reluctant to ask.

Adam had changed to a blue chambray shirt that made his eyes appear even greener than usual. She was keenly aware of her own rumpled condition and the perspiration beading her upper lip. It wasn't fair that men could look so good with so little effort. Adam needed a haircut and a shave, but even his shadowed cheeks and shaggy hair only added to his attractiveness, while her own hair was probably sticking out in a dozen directions.

He hooked a thumb into his belt, and she noticed he was wearing leather work gloves. The day he'd kissed her, his hands had been bare. She remembered their warmth against her skin with a rush of feeling.

Adam's voice snapped her back to the present. "Travis had to take Rory in to the clinic, so Kim stayed to watch the kids."

"Is Rory all right?" Emily asked, alarmed. "It's not a problem with the baby, is it?"

Adam glanced at David, who looked down at his feet. "She's probably fine. They just want to make sure."

"Would you please ask her to let me know if there's anything I can do?" Emily felt guilty for not calling Rory sooner.

Adam looked surprised. "I didn't know you two were friends."

"She's very nice. We had coffee the other day." Emily was reluctant to elaborate lest he suspect they'd discussed him. Which of course they had, but there was no reason for him to know.

His eyes narrowed slightly, deepening the creases at their outer corners. "Sure I'll tell her. Or you can call her yourself later on. Meanwhile, let's get these horses unloaded."

"Don't you want your money first?" Emily hurried to keep up with him as he headed toward the back of the trailer. "Is a personal check okay?"

"I trust you," Adam tossed over his shoulder.

A flush of pleasure warmed her cheeks at the undoubtedly impersonal compliment. In his business he must take checks all the time. How pathetic of her to find pleasure in something so generic. Setting her jaw, she brushed past him. "Let me show you the stalls we're using."

Once the horses were unloaded and settled into their new digs, Adam followed Emily back outside while her boy stayed in the stable. David's open interest surprised Adam, who'd expected the boy to act cool and indifferent. Instead he'd actually unbent enough to ask a few questions, and he'd listened attentively while Adam explained the routine the mare and the gelding were used to. Maybe there was hope for the boy yet, as long as he kept his distance from Kim.

"Thank you so much," Emily said quietly after Adam had replaced the ramp and closed up the trailer. "We'll take good care of them."

"If I wasn't reasonably sure of that, I wouldn't have sold them to you." He studied her face. There was a smudge of dirt on her cheek, and her lips were bare of artifice. He would have liked nothing more than to taste them, but he was painfully aware of their chaperon back in the stable with the horses.

And he had no idea whether she would welcome another pass from him. He knew how to run a ranch, but when it came to women, he felt clueless.

"I'll get your check," she said. "It's in the house."

Spirits lifting at the unexpected opportunity to test her interest, Adam followed her across the grass. When they reached the porch steps, she hesitated. "Would you like to come in?"

Her tone tickled him, as did her quick glance toward the stable. Good manners would force her to go through the motions of being polite, but he could sense her ambiguity.

"Oh, yeah, I'd like to come in," he drawled softly, encouraged by the way her hand tightened on the railing. When she nearly missed the first step, he caught her arm to steady her. Feeling her stiffen, he reluctantly let her go.

He'd never cared for the games that men and women played, but he enjoyed pushing Emily's buttons and watching her reaction. Her face was an emotional billboard.

Once again, her gaze slid past him. "David!" she called. "Want a snack?"

Adam nearly groaned aloud. Get lost, kid, he thought.

"No, thanks," the boy called from the doorway to the stable. "I'm going to brush out Puzzle's mane."

Yes! Adam quickly stifled his grin before Emily could notice. When she ascended the stairs, he followed her docilely. What would she do if he scooped her into his arms and carried her the rest of the way?

He had to be crazy to even think of touching her with her son in the vicinity. What kind of example would that be? Stay away from my daughter while I do my best to seduce your mother.

Right.

"I baked brownies," Emily said over her shoulder, "and I could brew some coffee if you'd like. It will only take a minute."

Watching the sway of her hips, Adam nearly missed her offer. "Sure," he managed to croak. "Whatever." He realized his response had been less than polite. "Sounds good," he added hastily, peeling off his gloves and stuffing them into his back pocket.

When she led the way inside, he was impressed with how she'd fixed up the living room. His own house had been a showplace when he'd first built it for Christie, but in the years since she'd left he hadn't bothered to update much of the inside décor, and he supposed it was beginning to look dated. Emily had turned this old place into a home, cozy and inviting.

"It looks real nice," he said when he realized she was watching for his reaction.

"Thank you." She gestured toward one bare wall while he doffed his hat and raked a hand through his hair. "I'm not done with it, by any means, but I wanted to take my time finding just the right local pictures and other pieces to finish it off."

"There's a painter in town who specializes in local scenery," Adam said.

"Does he have a gallery?" Emily asked. "Is it on the main street?"

"No, it's attached to his house out on Highway 86."

"And do you like his work?"

Her question surprised him. What did she care? "Most of it. If you're interested, I could take you by there sometime." Adam didn't bother to add that Wes had worked for the Running W until a fall from his horse had messed up his leg or that Adam had several of his paintings. Wes's talent had been wasted as a cowhand, anyway.

She hesitated, and he realized he was holding his breath. "That would be nice, if you can spare the time."

Relief surged through him, but he decided to back off while his luck held. "I'll call you this week, and we'll set it up."

She led the way through the small dining room to the outdated but spotlessly clean kitchen. "I'd hoped that David would take more of an interest in helping me decorate, but he still figures his dad will come to his senses and send for him."

The bitterness in her voice was impossible to ignore. "He'd rather live with his father?" Adam asked carefully.

Her head bobbed as she filled the coffee maker. "He'd rather live in L.A."

Adam couldn't begin to understand why anyone would choose smog and traffic over clean air and the room to move without bumping into someone. "Do you share custody?" He didn't want to pry, but he was finding that everything about Emily interested him. Bad sign.

She got out dishes and silver. "In theory. David is supposed to go back this summer, but his father is a busy, busy man."

"Not too busy to spend time with his own son?" Adam questioned, shocked at the idea. Maybe that was the boy's problem. Emily was no doubt a good mother, but a kid that age needed a firmer hand than she was likely to use.

She set down a painted metal tray with unnecessary force. Her eyes were stormy. "He'd better not be. David would be crushed if Stuart let him down. He's really been looking forward to it, and I know he feels like he's been replaced."

"How about you?" Adam asked, setting aside his hat. "Do you feel replaced, too?"

Her laugh was flat. "Not anymore."

The last thing Adam had intended was to be sidetracked into a discussion about her son and her ex. He'd wanted to make the most of these few minutes alone with her. Now he eased his way closer, effectively cornering her against the kitchen counter.

"The man's an idiot," he murmured.

Emily's eyes widened as his intention became obvious. She picked up a plate and extended it toward him.

"Have a brownie."

Adam's gaze slid to her mouth, and he was about to brace one hand beside her on the counter when he heard footsteps pounding up the front stairs. By the time David burst into the kitchen, Adam had taken a brownie from the plate and was about to bite into it.

David stopped in the doorway, his gaze

shifting back and forth like that of a bird dog sniffing out prey. "What's going on?" he demanded.

Emily's expression of wide-eyed innocence wouldn't have fooled a blind man. "I thought you weren't hungry."

"I changed my mind."

The look he gave Adam couldn't have been more territorial if he'd thrown a lasso around his mother. Apparently the tentative truce was over.

"Please go and wash up first," Emily said mildly.

With a last warning glare, David stomped out of the room as Adam chewed and swallowed his brownie.

"Well," she sighed as she pushed past him to pour the coffee, "that was fun."

Feeling surprisingly sympathetic to the boy's feelings, Adam helped himself to another frosted chocolate square. "He's just being protective," he said before he sank his teeth into it. On top of everything else, Emily was a damn fine cook.

Before he could tell her so, David was back.

"Let's sit down at the table like civilized folks," she said directly to him in a firm voice as she set everything on a tray. "Would you like some milk?"

David headed for the refrigerator as Adam took the tray from Emily and carried it to the dining room table.

"I'll get myself a soda," David said.

Emily looked flustered when Adam pulled out her chair, but she thanked him softly as she sat down. Deliberately Adam took the place directly across from her, leaving David no choice but to sit to the side. Two could play this game.

"How are the horses doing?" Emily asked as David helped himself to two brownies. Then he surprised Adam by passing the serving plate to him.

"I guess they're okay," David replied. "We're taking them out tomorrow, right?"

"After church." Emily stirred cream and sweetener into her coffee.

Adam expected him to argue, but he didn't. "Can I take this into my room and call Matt, the guy from school that you met?" he asked Emily. "He was talking about hanging out tonight."

She brightened noticeably. "Of course you can. I'm glad you're making friends."

David darted a glance at Adam, but he didn't say anything. Instead he wrapped his remaining brownie in a napkin and picked up his soda can. When he got to the doorway, he turned.

"Thanks for bringing over the horses," he told Adam. "And I hope Rory will be okay."

Adam nodded slowly. "You're welcome. And I'll pass on your good wishes."

After David had disappeared down the hall, shutting his bedroom door behind him, Emily looked at Adam with a defensive expression. "He's a good boy," she said as the sound of music came from his room. It wasn't nearly as loud as Kim sometimes played hers.

"Maybe so." Adam was fully aware that he wasn't helping his own cause a bit. "But I'm still not letting him near Kim. He's a teenager and a city kid besides."

"What's *that* supposed to mean?" Emily demanded hotly.

Adam knew he'd said too much. He slid back his chair and got to his feet. "Give it time."

"How much time?" she shot back at him as she, too, stood up.

He grinned, trying to lighten the suddenly charged atmosphere. "About five years ought to do it."

Chapter Ten

Emily was tempted to protest Adam's declaration that it would be five years before he would let her son near his daughter, but instead she decided to let it go for now.

"What? No comment?" he asked when she began clearing off the table.

Emily paused to give him a level stare. "Either your mind is made up and nothing will change it, or you're a fair man who won't pass judgment on my son without getting to know him first."

Adam's eyes narrowed and his expression iced over, but she'd had enough. Head high, she carried the laden tray back to the kitchen. He didn't try to stop her, but after she'd set it down on the tile counter, she spun back around and nearly collided with him.

Startled, she folded her arms and braced herself for another tirade. Adam studied her with a considering expression.

"You play dirty," he said.

"When it comes to my son's welfare, I don't *play* at all." Her temper rose, and she tried to duck around him, but he blocked her escape by shifting to the side. Unwilling to bob back and forth, she settled for a chilly glare.

Adam stood rubbing his jaw for a long moment. "Does the boy want a job?" he asked.

"What do you mean?" Emily waved her hand in the direction of David's room. "The *boy* is a high school student, remember?" What kind of game was Adam playing now?

"Saturdays until school is out, full-time for the summer."

Emily's spurt of interest in the idea was immediately quashed by disappointment. "He's going to L.A. in June to stay with his father." At least he was if Stuart could spare the time.

Adam shrugged. "Okay. He can start before he leaves. If he does a decent job, I'll keep a spot open for him."

"Are you kidding me?" she demanded. "Because if you are, you're not being very funny."

"I'm making you a serious offer."

"But why?" she had to ask. "You don't even like him, and you don't want him anywhere near your daughter." Could Adam possibly think of this as a way to get on *Emily's* good side? She doubted that part-time and summer jobs were thick on the ground around here, but she wasn't sure she cared for the idea of her son working in a hostile environment. As far as the idea of Adam trying to get to her, that was something she'd have to think about later, when he wasn't looming over her, so close she could see each spiky black lash that framed the clear green of his eyes.

"As you pointed out, I don't *know* him," Adam contradicted, ignoring her comment about Kim, "so maybe I'm trying to correct that."

Emily hadn't dreamed that he would even respond to her statement, let alone act on it. Perhaps she'd misjudged him. "David can ride a horse, but he's not all that competent yet," she confessed.

"If he works for me, he'll learn."

She winced at the mental image of her son chasing cattle through the brush as he clung to the saddle horn and tried desperately to spin a lasso over his head—or riding a bronc and getting thrown. "What would he be doing?" She leaned against the counter, folding her arms across her chest and struggling for calm. Just being near Adam, breathing him in, set her nerves tingling with awareness. He smelled like soap and outdoors and hard work, but not in an unpleasant way. Far from it.

He shrugged. "David would be doing whatever needs to be done. Don't worry. I'll make sure he's well supervised. I'm not about to turn a green kid loose on his own. A ranch can be a dangerous place, but I wouldn't risk your son's welfare, Emily."

Hearing her name spoken in his deep, sensual voice sent a shiver of reaction dancing up her spine. Staying focused on the subject at hand wasn't easy when he stood so close, his gaze locked on hers. Not even when the subject was her son.

What kind of mother was she? She opened her mouth to refuse before she could give in to temptation.

"I'll pay him a flat hourly wage," Adam continued. He named a figure that sounded ridiculously low. "Unless you don't want him to work? Maybe he doesn't need the money."

She straightened away from the counter. She'd always done her best to teach David about responsibility, despite their affluent lifestyle. He'd asked her about getting a job so he could save for a car, but she'd stalled, worried that his grades might suffer. In some ways, having him work right next door would be ideal.

She decided to ignore Adam's comment about the money. "What about Kim?"

"She's going to be busy helping Rory with the new baby." A flash of something indecipherable crossed his face. "My daughter doesn't take a great deal of interest in the day-to-day routine of running a ranch."

"That must be disappointing," Emily said.

He gave her a wry grin. "That may change in time. Meanwhile, I'm finding out that the minds of teenage girls are occupied with clothes, makeup, boys—" As abruptly as it had appeared, his smile faded. He cleared his throat. "I'll make sure that neither one of them will have time for fraternization." He glanced over his shoulder in the direction of David's room. "Shall I talk to him while I'm here?"

Emily had no idea how David might react to the offer, but she suspected he was counting on his father letting him stay for the entire summer. "Let me think about it first," she told Adam. "We'll get back to you in a couple of days, okay?"

"Sure." Adam took a step back, and disappointment welled up inside her as he picked up his hat. "I'd better be going."

"Thank you again for bringing the horses over and for the job offer." She laced her fingers together in front of her, determined not to let her feelings show. Had she really thought he might try something with David right down the hall? For a variety of reasons, she should be relieved that he hadn't.

"Walk me out?" Adam's gaze slid away from hers as he turned the brim of his hat around and around in his hands. If she hadn't known better, she might have thought he was nervous. It was more likely that he was having second thoughts about his rash offer. Still, pleasure at his request flooded through her, and she hoped she wasn't blushing.

"Of course." She kept her voice brisk, just in case she'd misinterpreted his suggestion. "I want to check on the horses again, anyway, and the kittens." David's bedroom window was on the far side of the house from where the truck was parked, so he wouldn't even notice Adam's departure.

Oh, how wanton her thoughts were when Adam came around!

"Perhaps I'd better check the horses with you," he said when they'd gone down the front steps and were crossing the yard together. "Just to make sure they're settling in okay."

Emily sneaked a glance up at him, and her heart nearly skipped a beat at the way he was looking at her. "Okay."

They walked to the stable in silence. As her eyes adjusted to the dimness, she saw Puzzle raise his head, ears pricked forward. Adam went over and talked quietly to the gelding as though he was saying goodbye to an old friend. While he repeated the ritual with Shyla, Emily took the opportunity to visit Penny and her little family and to will herself to relax. The kittens, two orange and white, a small black runt and a calico like its mother, were all sleeping. Penny's head popped up and her whiskers quivered as she gazed at Emily. After a moment, the cat yawned and closed her eyes.

Wishing she could absorb some of the animal's calm, Emily leaned against the wall and took a deep breath. She had to stop thinking about kissing Adam, she lectured herself sternly as she pressed her palms to her burning cheeks. What was wrong with her? She'd moved to Colorado determined to steer clear of romantic entanglements, and now the first man to show an interest had her emotions in a tailspin!

She heard a noise behind her. Adam put his hands on her shoulders and squeezed gently. If the motion was meant to soothe her jangled nerves, it had the opposite effect.

"You're tense." Slowly he turned her face to him.

Their gazes met and held as the awareness between them built up until it was nearly tangible. Resisting the urge to moisten her dry lips, she studied him silently.

"Emily?" His tone lacked its usual confidence. "Am I alone here?"

Her eyes widened. "What do you mean?"

Tension drew the skin tight across his cheekbones, giving him the look of a predator. "You must know that I want you."

"N-no," she stammered, stunned by his bluntness. "I didn't—"

"Didn't what? Think that kiss we shared meant anything?" he said. "Maybe you figured me for a guy who makes passes at women he's not attracted to, just to stay in practice or something." His tone was light, but he watched her intently.

"No, I didn't think that." Her mind refused to function at more than a basic level. His nearness was scrambling her senses, his words stirring an answering hunger in her, even as her practical side was reminding her that there were so many, many reasons why getting any further involved with Adam had to be a colossally unwise idea.

"Maybe it just didn't mean anything to you," he suggested.

"What about David?" she asked, ignoring his last remark as his grip shifted to her waist and he drew her closer. "And Kim?"

Adam's broad chest expanded on a deep sigh, but he didn't release her. "Can't you stop being a mother for a moment and just be a woman? They're our children. We don't answer to them."

Part of Emily was tempted to debate that, but the huskiness of his voice and the warmth of his hands were weaving a sensual spell around her. "I doubt you ever forget you're a dad," she murmured.

He rolled his eyes. "Maybe I don't, but right now it's not the first thing on my mind."

The memory of his mouth on hers was too much for Emily to ignore any longer. Resisting temptation was beyond her. "You're not alone in this," she admitted in a ragged whisper.

Passion flared in his eyes as her meaning sank in. His fingers flexed on her waist.

"Ever since the last time, I've wanted to do this again," he admitted, lowering his head.

Sliding her hands up the hard wall of his chest, Emily tipped back her head to meet him halfway. This time there was no hesitation, no time for her to draw back. He pulled her flush against his unyielding body as his open mouth covered hers in a searing kiss.

Heat burst inside her. The pit of her stomach seemed to fall away and she melted like hot wax, her whole being responding to the urgency that flared between them like a match tossed on gasoline.

She twined her arms around his neck, her breasts flattening against his chest. Her knees trembled; her heart stuttered. He groaned, a low rumble of need. A storm of passion, stronger than Emily would have believed herself capable of feeling, swept over her, blotting out everything else. Adam surrounded her with his arms and his desire. Helplessly, mindlessly, she surrendered.

When he ended the kiss, she cuddled close, pressing her hot cheek against his thundering heartbeat. His arms were like steel bands. Without their support, she might have fallen. Her legs were that weak.

The only sounds were their ragged breathing and a horse's restless pawing. Emily felt deliciously languid, snuggled against his warmth, her eyes squeezed shut. Her nipples throbbed, and the feel of his arousal made her want to rub against him in sensual abandon.

"Emily?" His voice was less than a whisper. His breath stirred her hair, and then his arms fell to his sides.

"Hmm?" She tightened her grip around his neck and looked up at him through the protective screen of her lashes. Even though she struggled to keep reality at bay, it refused to be ignored.

Adam cupped her elbows gently and eased her away from him. "How long before David gets curious and comes out here?"

She stiffened with shock. What was she doing? What was she *thinking?* She scrambled back so fast that she stumbled against an old wooden chair and would have fallen if his hands hadn't been quick. Her expression must have mirrored the pure horror she felt at the idea of being discovered with her mouth fused to his and their bodies welded together. His grin was rueful.

"You look guilty as sin."

Her hands went to her hair, and then she remembered that she'd worn it loose. She patted the front of her blouse, checking for buttons that might need attention. "I'm not, I didn't—" she stammered.

He leaned down and pressed a brief, firm kiss to her half-parted lips, straightening again before she could respond. "No, we didn't," he agreed. "I'm painfully aware of that, believe me." He shifted, drawing her attention to the altered fit of his snug jeans. "But don't think for a moment that anything would have stopped us if we had been truly alone."

She started to protest his certainty, but her sense of honesty prevailed. Would she have, just like that? On a musty blanket in the tack room or an empty stall? Of course she wouldn't, not with her son in the house. But if he *wasn't* here?

"I'd better go." Adam lifted his hat and raked his free hand through his hair before he turned away.

It was all Emily could do to keep herself from grabbing at him like some poor, desperate groupie. That pathetic image and the risk of detection finally snapped her out of the lovesick fog that had enveloped her.

What had she been thinking, plastering herself up against Adam like that? Clinging to him. Had she lost her mind? For a timeless moment, she stood with her fingertips pressed against her lips as she willed her racing heart to slow.

By the time she'd collected her wits and caught up with Adam, he was sliding the metal ramp back into the trailer. He moved with economy and pure masculine grace. When he was done, he straightened up and watched her, his jaw set as he peeled off his work gloves.

"If you still want me to, I can take you over to see Wes's paintings. How about Tuesday afternoon?"

Paintings? It took Emily a moment to switch gears. By then a dark flush had stained his cheeks as though he had already anticipated her refusal.

"I'd like that," she replied hastily. She had to be crazy to voluntarily spend more time with him. Blame it on that hint of uncertainty she'd glimpsed beneath his confident veneer. Animal magnetism she had no problem resisting, but she'd always been a sucker for vulnerability.

She nearly grinned at his double take. This was a man who'd apparently developed the expectation of rejection into an art form.

He blinked a couple of times. "Great," he said, glancing up at the house. When he looked back at Emily, his gaze swooped unerringly to her mouth. "I'll check back with you about the time."

Leaving without touching her again wasn't easy for Adam, but the idea of putting on a peepshow for her son held little appeal. They were damn lucky the kid hadn't walked in on them in the stable.

Jaw clenched against the need still grinding inside him when he got behind the wheel, Adam steered the pickup in a wide circle. What was she thinking as she wiggled her fingers in a gesture of farewell? When he drove back down her driveway, his gaze stayed glued to the retreating image of her in his side mirror until she finally turned away.

Emily Major was fast becoming an obsession with him, and their latest encounter had done nothing to diminish his growing hunger for her.

Emily took a deep breath as she walked back into the house. Maybe she should have refused Adam's job offer outright, but what if Kim mentioned it to David? He'd be upset that his mother had made the decision without telling him, even if he wasn't interested in accepting.

Through his closed bedroom door she could hear him on the phone. At first she thought he must be talking to Stuart, but then she remembered that he'd said he was going to call Matt from school.

The door burst open as she raised her hand to knock.

"Hey," David said, looking startled. His altered appearance was still a jolt. He looked so…normal. "Winchester gone?" he asked, his gaze darting past her.

"Mr. Winchester to you," she corrected gently. "Yes, he left. But there's something I need to talk to you about."

David's expression turned wary. "Can it wait? Matt's coming by to pick me up."

"Where are you going?" she asked.

He shrugged. "Just around."

Emily folded her arms across her chest, leaned against the opposite wall and waited. He'd been in enough trouble back home that she felt justified.

He sighed. "We're going to play hoops at the school."

"Be home by ten," Emily said.

The protest she expected didn't come. Instead he shrugged. "Yeah, whatever. Matt will be here any minute."

"Mr. Winchester's offered you a job at his ranch," she said before he could shut his door again. "After school until summer and then full-time. Are you interested?"

"But I'll be going to Dad's when school's out," he protested. "I can get work there."

"If you do okay, Mr. Winchester said he'd keep a spot open till you get back." She hoped she wouldn't have to explain how the offer had come about in the first place.

"What would I do?" he asked. "I sure don't know anything about ranching."

"If you're interested, you can ask him yourself."

They both heard the sound of an engine outside and then a door slamming.

David's gaze darted past her. "That's Matt. I gotta go."

Emily stepped aside. "Just think about it," she suggested, relieved that he hadn't rejected the idea outright.

On Tuesday Adam planned on getting Emily back from Wes's with plenty of time to spare before school got out for the day. When she opened the door, he had the choice of either stepping back from the door or hauling her into his arms. For the time being, discretion won out.

Although she had pinned her hair in a soft knot on top of her head, several strands had already worked their way free to curl around her face. Sunglasses with light-green lenses perched on her nose. A loose-fitting sundress bared her arms to the day's heat. The V-neck, edged with lace, revealed a ladylike hint of cleavage, but the skirt hung to midcalf and covered—in his opinion—too much of her long, delicious legs.

Adam swallowed his disappointment. "You look like a photo from a fashion magazine," he said, "cool as a drink of water."

She was holding a straw purse that matched her sandals. Small, white hoops danced at her earlobes. "Thank you. Are you sure you can spare the time for this? You're not too busy?"

"I hope I never get that busy," he muttered fervently as he led her around to the passenger side of his truck. "Besides, Wes is expecting us." Adam's own concession to the warm day had been to roll back the sleeves of his shirt and swap his Resistol for a baseball cap.

She let him assist her into the passenger seat, her hand warm in his, and then she smoothed her skirt down over her knees. "It's nice of you to drive me," she said primly.

Adam wasn't sure how to answer, so he didn't say anything until he was settled behind the wheel. Did she look on this merely as a neighborly favor? He caught her nibbling her lip, and a little confidence seeped back, along with a rush of heat. Was the care she'd taken with her appearance an indication that she returned his interest? He wished he was better at reading women, but he'd never been good at that.

"How are the horses doing?" he asked as he started the engine. The two Appies had glanced up from their grazing at the sound of his truck pulling in. "Have you ridden them yet?"

Emily pushed her sunglasses back up her nose and then she folded her hands demurely on her purse. A smile curved her lips, tempting Adam to lean over and kiss her just to see how she'd react. And, of course, because he was dying to taste her soft mouth. "Oh, yes. David and I have been out twice, on Sunday after church and again yesterday. They're both wonderfully trained."

"Well, thank you, ma'am." The unexpected compliment pleased him. "Are you going riding again today when your boy gets home from school?" he probed, feeling about as subtle as a poker player with a good hand and a smirk.

The loose strands of hair stirred in the breeze from the open window as she shook her head. "David's going with Matt to watch some calf roping, and they're stopping at the drive-in for burgers afterward. I'm told that's the local teen hangout."

Adam struggled not to let his elation show. "Are they heading out to Montgomery's spread?"

"How did you know?"

"Kim's going with a couple of other girls."

"I know it's a school night," Emily said, "but I'm so glad he's making friends that I hated to say no." She shot him a glance. "I'm a little surprised that Kim is going."

Adam wasn't used to anyone questioning the way he was raising his daughter. "I suppose you think I'm some kind of ogre because I don't let her run wild," he said testily.

"I'm sorry. I'm really not in a position to criticize anyone." Her voice was soft. "I've made mistakes."

As quickly as it had risen, Adam's temper faded. He'd been incredibly lucky with Kim so far, even though she seemed annoyed with him lately. "Parenting isn't an exact science. I guess the trick is to learn from our mistakes and move on."

Emily sighed "Yes, of course you're right. Is the job offer for David still good?"

An old Plymouth with fins and two-tone paint came up behind them fast and swung out to pass. "Damned idiot," Adam muttered, tapping the brakes when the other driver cut back in too closely. The idea of Kim riding in a car with someone like that twisted a hard knot in his gut.

"Is David interested?" he asked.

Emily fiddled with the strap to her purse. "He has visions of spending the entire summer in California, but it's not going to happen. He'll be there whenever you want."

Adam had already had second—and third—thoughts about his rash offer, but he wasn't about to go back on it now. That wasn't the way he operated. "I'm not sure about the rest of this week. Have him call me."

Adam spent the next few minutes pointing out local scenery. In too short a time for him, they arrived at the small house where Wes had insisted on moving when it became clear that sitting a horse was in his past. Adam had offered him a place to stay at the ranch for as long as the old coot wanted. When he refused, Adam tried to buy this place for him and ran smack up against Wes's stiff-necked pride. Working with the local banker behind Wes's back, Adam had at least been able to guarantee a mortgage with easy terms. All three Winchesters had converted the attached garage into a studio.

"We're here," he said unnecessarily as he turned into the driveway. "Don't feel obligated to buy anything. If Wes thought you were giving him charity, he'd refuse to take your money."

"The Brentwood house was full of valuable art pieces I had no say in picking out," Emily replied. "Don't worry. Nothing comes into this home that I don't love."

Her remark fueled Adam's curiosity about her marriage, but he ignored it. If she left empty-handed, he'd sneak back later and tell Wes she'd decided on something after all.

After Adam had made introductions, Wes took them to the studio. Adam stayed out of the way while Emily looked through the stacks of canvasses, asking Wes about several of them.

"It's so hard to choose," she said. "They're all wonderful, but these are the two I have to have." She'd chosen two large paintings, one a prairie scene filled with a riot of wildflowers and the other a lone rider darkly silhouetted against the vivid streaks of a sunset. Cheeks pink, she glanced at Adam. "This one reminds me a little of you."

He took a closer look at the picture. Despite the vivid background colors, Wes had managed to capture a sense of brooding isolation in the figure's posture. Was that how she saw Adam, as someone to be pitied because he was alone? "The hat's wrong," he said brusquely. "I never wear a Stetson."

Wes ignored his remark. "I'll have them matted and framed by next week," he promised Emily with a twinkle in his eye. "Why don't you leave this big lug behind and come back on your own? I don't bite."

Emily returned his grin. "I might do just that."

"Misplace your store-bought teeth?" Adam demanded, pleased to find his old friend in high spirits. He'd tried to apologize for not coming out in a while, but Wes had brushed aside his words, claiming to have been too busy to make time for any company other than the attractive female kind.

Emily had blushed at his teasing leer, making Adam wonder if she was really unaware of her own beauty. What kind of job had her ex-husband done on her ego before he'd tossed her aside? It was one more question that would have to wait for an answer.

Wes led them back to the house, where he insisted on serving coffee you could stand a spoon in and cookies from the new bakery. He'd been a fixture at the ranch since Adam's old man had been in charge, and Emily's presence today was all the excuse Wes needed to recall one story after another that placed Adam in the role of comic relief.

"If you still worked for me, I'd fire you," he grumbled while Emily laughed over a particularly unflattering tale from his boyhood. He and Travis had sneaked a bottle of cheap wine from the house. If the old man had caught them, there would have been hell to pay, so it was Wes who held their heads and sympathized while they puked their guts out after foolishly downing the whole bottle between them. Struggling to hide their misery from their sharp-eyed father had been a powerful lesson in moderation that Adam had never forgotten.

"Poor Travis was as green as a spring frog the next morning," Wes recalled with a shake of his head. "You weren't much better. Man, did I feel sorry for the two of you."

"And you covered for us mending fence," Adam remembered. "Did your share of the work and most of ours so the old man wouldn't suspect."

He and Wes exchanged a look of understanding. "You were good boys, the lot of you. Full of mischief, like any young'uns, but still just boys. Garth tended to forget that."

Adam glanced at Emily, who was watching

the pair of them with a thoughtful expression. "The old man did the best he could with us after our mother cut out," he said defensively. "He didn't want to raise any weaklings."

"You were kids who'd lost your momma," Wes argued back as he gripped his cane and got to his feet. "You needed—" He cleared his throat. "Well, no point in riding that range again now, I don't s'pose. I suspect you two've got better things to do than listen to the ramblings of a dried-up old cowboy like me."

"You're a talented artist," Emily replied with a snap to her voice. "If my friends from L.A. could see your work, they'd pick you clean. I'll be back for one of those mountain scenes when I get the chance."

Wes flushed pinker than a baby with a sunburn. "Well, thank you. Adam, your taste in women has improved, I'll give you that."

Before he could think of a reply to that sally, Wes turned to Emily and asked about her work. Briefly she described what she did.

"Sounds like I'm not the only artist in this room," Wes said. "Maybe I'll visit *your* studio one day."

"Come by anytime." Emily was obviously pleased by his interest.

Adam realized he'd dropped the ball there. He'd have to ask for a tour one day soon.

Before they left a few moments later, Emily planted a kiss on Wes's leathery cheek. As platonic as the gesture had to be, Adam felt a jab of jealousy, or maybe it was just envy that the old man had gotten to loop an arm around her for a moment. Adam's arms felt damned empty these days and so did the long nights he lay awake.

"Thank you for being so nice to him," he told Emily on the way back home. "He's had a difficult time."

"He's quite a character," she replied, "and it's obvious that he thinks highly of you."

"Not so highly that he'd skip the story about the heifer that shoved me into a cow pie when I had on my best suit!" Adam drawled. "Or his comments about my high school dating experiences."

"Those sounded pretty tame," she teased.

"For me, dating back in high school *was* tame." He'd been clumsy, awkward and painfully shy. "When I tried talking to girls, my tongue tied itself into a knot."

She tilted her head as she studied his profile. "I'll bet they were all dying for you to notice them."

"And why would you say that?" he probed lightly. "Trying to butter me up? I'm already set to hire your kid."

Her lashes fluttered prettily, reminding him of the one-handed okay sign Wes had given him behind her back when they'd first arrived.

"I have no reason to butter you up, as you say," she denied, twiddling with a strand of her hair. "If you didn't have a mirror in high school, that was your own problem."

She must have immediately realized the implication behind her remark, because her hands went to her cheeks and she groaned. Adam didn't bother to hide his pleased smirk.

"Just because I find you attractive doesn't mean I'm interested in getting involved with you," she exclaimed with a prissy lift of her chin.

He put his hand on her knee. "I'd say we're already involved."

She used two fingers on his wrist to move his hand back to the seat between them. "We're just neighbors."

"You kiss all your neighbors?" he asked.

A smile tugged at the corners of Emily's mouth. "Well, all but old Mrs. Campbell. She has a mustache."

Something he hadn't felt in a long time swelled in his chest. Happiness. The simple, uncomplicated enjoyment of a woman's company.

"Ah, yes," he teased, "but I'm the one you find attractive."

Her smile widened. "I'm not blind, Winchester, just choosy."

His mind went blank. Before he could recover from a surge of pure pleasure, she changed the subject. "So what happened to Wes? How was he hurt?"

A sudden rush of memories tightened Adam's grip on the steering wheel. "It was deep winter and the day was bitter cold. Wes was riding out to bring me some urgent news. His horse went down on some ice, rolled over on him before he could get clear and pretty much crushed his pelvis. Took us a while to find him." He didn't add that Wes had been coming to warn him of Christie's imminent departure—from the ranch and from Adam's life.

"How awful," Emily said. "Can he ride at all?"

Adam shook his head. "As you saw, he walks with a cane now, but at least he's out of the chair. That was when Rory took him a set of oil paints and got him started."

"You all must care a lot about him."

It wasn't a question, but he answered, anyway. Kim had told him during an argument— flung the words at him, actually—that he had no feelings, so he was trying to open up, but it wasn't easy.

"I guess you could say that I love him and not be wrong." His voice hitched, making him feel like ten kinds of a fool. He stared straight ahead, jaw locked. To his surprise, he felt a touch on his thigh. He glanced down to see Emily's hand resting there. For an instant the thread of their conversation drained away, along with the rush of blood leaving his brain for points south.

"If the accident hadn't happened, he might never have discovered his talent," she pointed out softly.

"I hadn't thought of that." Adam's load of guilt shifted just a little.

"Things happen for a reason."

He glanced at her and swallowed hard. He wanted to turn down the nearest side road, stop the truck and pull her beneath him. He desperately craved the connection. Stronger, though, was the urge to protect her, even from himself. That was damned scary. "Do you really believe in fate?"

She pursed her lips as she considered his question. "Sometimes. My marriage was less than ideal and not something I'd ever try again, but I have David, so I guess I'd have to say that, yes, I do. What about you?"

He was surprised to realize they'd reached her turnoff. "I guess I haven't thought about it from that angle too much, but I can't imagine a life without my daughter." He drove slowly toward her house so he wouldn't raise a cloud of dust. Perhaps it was time to lighten the mood and distract them both.

He braked the pickup and turned to her, resting his arm against the steering wheel. "So marriage is out, huh?" he asked past the sudden tightness in his throat. "How about if we just have a blazing affair?"

Chapter Eleven

Assuming that Adam was joking, Emily meant to give him a flip answer to his question, an answer designed to show him that she, too, could kid about having an affair. Before she could speak, she saw that his expression had turned serious. Watchful. Her teasing response died on her tongue.

"Dammit," he rasped, "when you look at me like that, I can't think straight."

"Like what?" she asked.

"All wide-eyed and sexy as hell."

She swallowed hard. Sexy? *Her?* Awareness flared between them as quickly, as easily, as a match tossed in dry grass. His eyes darkened as though he could read the hungry message in hers. His hands went to her shoulders, his fingers flexing, but his attempt to drag her closer was hindered by their seat belts. With a succinct muttered curse, he freed himself while she fumbled helplessly with the buckle on hers. Finally he brushed her hand aside. She was about to make a nervous comment about modern technology interfering with romantic spontaneity, but a glance at his face changed her mind. When was the last time anyone had desired her with such untamed ferocity, such naked lust? Not for years.

The second she was free from the passive restraint, Adam cupped her face in his hands, his thumbs tipping up her chin, and covered her mouth in a searing kiss, a heated claiming that made her tremble. He must have felt it, because he broke the intimate contact.

"Did I hurt you?" His gritty voice was laced with concern, his brows bunched into a frown as he studied her.

"No." She lifted a shaky hand to his hard jaw, a thrill going through her at the feel of his skin beneath her palm. "No," she said again.

"David?" he rasped, stroking her hair.

Understanding his meaning, she shifted her gaze to the clock on his dash. "Even if he were to come straight home, he wouldn't be here for another hour."

"You're sure?"

Was he still talking about David or something else entirely? Either way, her answer was the same. She lifted her chin. "Positive."

His intimidating expression relaxed into a dazzling smile, his hot gaze sliding to her mouth. "Good." He gave her hair a gentle tug before he straightened and eased the truck back into gear to complete the short trip down the driveway. Feeling incredibly brave, she slid over and rested her hand on the hard muscle of his thigh. It flexed as he braked in front of the door and killed the engine.

Adam turned to her silently, waiting, and she had to swallow hard. She knew what it would mean if she invited him in and had already made the decision in her heart. She was half in love with this man she barely knew, and her pulse was pounding as though she'd climbed onto a thrill ride and was already racing down the metal track.

Emily took a deep breath. She lifted Adam's baseball cap off his dark hair and set it on the dash. Surprise flared in his eyes. She leaned close, pressing her mouth to his. When she would have straightened, he caught the back of her head in one big hand and deepened the kiss.

The touch of his lips and tongue sent tendrils of desire curling deep inside her, and she had to choke back a whimper of pure pleasure. She flattened her hand against his chest, and beneath her palm his heart thudded, strong and steady. She felt wild and out of control yet strangely safe with him.

For years she'd let family and duty set her course. Today, this moment, was just for her. Pure selfish lust.

When he nibbled a path along her jaw, igniting the sensitive nerves, she pulled away. "Come inside," she invited, well past any pretense of coffee or a cool drink. She wanted him, so let him know it. Let him see it in her face and feel it in her touch as she stroked his forearm. The dark, springy hair tickled the pads of her fingers, hinted at sensations yet to be explored.

"Yes, please," he said softly, shoving open his door and urging her out after him. When her feet touched the ground, he curled his arm around her shoulders and pulled her close to bury his face in her hair. He lifted his head as Monty came down the steps, tail wagging.

Absently Emily patted the dog's head.

"Good boy," she murmured a little breathlessly.

When she straightened, Adam leaned over to kiss her again. Monty let out a yip and Adam smiled against her lips. Holding hands, they went into her house as Monty lay back down on the porch.

Emily would have led Adam right to her bedroom, but he stopped her. "You need to know this isn't a sudden thing with me," he said, cupping her face in his hands. "I've wanted you since the day you ran me down at the feed store."

Emily wondered if he felt he had to say that. She refused to speculate on his feelings or what the future might hold. She was breaking out, being selfish, and it felt damn good.

"You tried to run me off," she reminded him.

He shrugged. "Maybe I was in denial."

She didn't want to talk. When he looked at her as he was doing now, she could barely breathe. Daringly she reached up and pulled open the top snap of his shirt. Before she could continue, he captured her hands in his and brought them to his mouth, kissing her knuckles.

Adam studied her flushed cheeks, her slumberous eyes and lips that were slightly swollen from the kisses they'd already shared. Had he lost his mind? He should be after her land, not her body, but he couldn't, wouldn't deny himself what she seemed so willing to give.

This time when she led him down the hall, he didn't try to slow her down, nor did he do more than glance at his surroundings. He was vaguely aware that her room was finished in light colors and scrupulously neat, but that was all.

"You must think I do this kind of thing all the time," Emily said, and he recognized the sudden hesitation in her tone. The idea that she might yet change her mind was enough to draw his attention back to her, only to her.

Wrapping his arms around her, he kissed her hungrily. "All I've been thinking is how lucky I am," he said when they came up for air. "You're everything a man could want." Before he could say anything else, she reached up and pulled his head back down. Her mouth was hot and moist, her curves fitting against him as snugly as though their two bodies were adjoining pieces of the same puzzle. The attraction he'd been struggling to control slammed into him, driving out rational thought. With a harsh groan of surrender, he bent down and scooped her into his arms.

Her startled gasp as he lifted her effortlessly off the floor stopped him cold, but her lips curved in obvious approval and her throaty purr as she stroked his chest made him feel ten feet tall. Sucking in a deep breath, he did his best to slow the pace.

Emily's busy hands did their best to shatter his control, teasing and tempting him until need took over.

By the time their clothing was scattered on the floor, Emily had managed to banish the last whisper of hesitation and to simply feast her senses on the man she was about to take as a lover. Hard work had sculpted his physique in a way that no gym or personal trainer ever could. Muscles roped his arms and shaped his powerful shoulders. His back was a work of art despite several long scars. His chest, when he turned, was wide, with a dusting of dark hair that drew her gaze downward to his narrow waist and beyond.

"I knew you'd be lovely all over," he murmured, studying her openly. The approval on his face went a long way toward soothing her most basic insecurities.

Emily resisted the urge to cover herself or to stammer out a polite thank-you. Instead she continued to look at him. His skin, when she touched him, was hot and smooth, his scent clean and masculine.

His desire for her was obvious, and his hands on her when they lay together were clever enough to stroke away the last bit of awkwardness between them. By the time he pulled her beneath his powerful body, she was wild with need, and he was trembling with the effort of holding back. Despite the intensity of their joining, Adam managed to find the last shred of control, letting her spin into oblivion before he found his own release in her arms.

By the time his breathing had slowed and his heart was no longer beating as though it would explode from his chest, Adam could already sense her retreat. All he wanted was to cuddle her close and doze like a cat in the sun, but despite the warmth of the afternoon, the air in Emily's bedroom was definitely turning cool.

He shifted to his side so he could see her. She lay with her face turned away, the sheet pulled up over her hip, and his first thought was that he'd somehow disappointed or hurt her. Then he remembered the way she'd come apart in his arms, sobbing his name. Unless she was a hell of an actor, she'd been with him every step of the way.

"Emily?" He closed his hand over her shoulder, feeling her stiffen. Oh, man, he hoped she wasn't crying. Whenever Kim cried, it tore him up inside.

To his relief she rolled onto her back, pulling the sheet even higher so that it hid her breasts from his interested gaze. At least her eyes were dry, not tear-stained as he'd feared.

"Yes?" Her voice was distant, and she looked at the ceiling rather than at him. Not a good sign.

"Are you okay?" he asked, contentment fading.

"Of course." She turned her head so their gazes met. Her smile trembled at the corners. "I'm fine."

Fine. It was less than he'd hoped for. Propping himself up on his elbow, he stroked his finger down her cheek. At least she didn't flinch away.

"I know this all happened pretty fast," he said haltingly, inadequately, "but I'm glad to be here with you."

Emily sat up, still holding the sheet firmly in place. "We'd better get dressed," she said, glancing at the clock on the night stand. "Just in case—"

"Yeah, sure." Adam had forgotten about her son, about the real world, the moment he'd exited his pickup. Emily had already snagged her bra from the floor where one of them had tossed it and was putting it on. He would have liked to watch her dress, but that would have to wait for the next time. If there was another time. Feeling helpless, he began gathering up his clothes. There were things he wanted to say to her and to hear her say, but they would have to wait.

After Adam drove off, his frustration obvious, Emily rushed back inside to make the bed and to erase any other possible indication of what had taken place. David probably wouldn't be home for hours, but as soon as she'd straightened up the bedroom, she stripped off her clothes again and stepped into the shower in the connecting bathroom. Only while the spray washed away the last remnants of what she and Adam had shared did she let herself think about his words after he'd led her by hand out to his truck and given her a thorough kiss.

"We'll slow things down, if that's what you want," he said, his expression almost grim, "but don't think for a moment that you're going to pull away from me. It's too late for that, for both of us."

She hadn't replied, and he hadn't seemed to expect her to. Instead of kissing her again, he'd gotten into his truck and driven away without a backward glance.

Hadn't she sworn off forceful men before she moved here? Adam had certainly changed his tune since all he'd wanted was her land.

She'd been about to turn off the shower, but the thought froze her hand in midair. What if this was just a new plan to get it? Pursue her, break her heart and send her crying back to L.A.?

Heedless of her nakedness, Emily turned off the water and sat down on the edge of the tub. Before he'd sold her the property, Mr. Johnson had made her promise that she would never resell it to the Winchesters. The old man had refused to tell her why. Perhaps he was getting senile. Determined to put down new roots in a place that would be safe for David, with no idea who owned the land surrounding hers on three sides, she had reluctantly agreed to the unusual condition. With nothing in writing, it wasn't legally binding, but she'd given her word, and she felt honor bound to keep it.

If Adam knew how she felt, would he still be interested in her?

A sudden chill made her shiver. Drying off with a thick Egyptian-cotton towel she'd brought with her from the house in Brentwood, she realized that for the time being at least, discouraging Adam was the last thing she wanted to do.

By the time David got home, bursting in the front door with a grin on his face and a smear of dirt across one cheek, she was watching television as calmly as if her day had been strictly routine.

"Have a good time?" she asked after he'd greeted her on his way to the kitchen and returned to flop into a chair with a can of cold soda in his hand.

"Yeah. It was fun." He took a long swallow, and she noticed that his shoulders were starting to fill out and his face was getting tanned. "Some of the kids are pretty cool," he added.

"I'm glad you're making friends," Emily replied. Perhaps between that and working for Adam, he'd be too busy to miss California.

He shifted in the chair, picking at the fabric covering the arm. "Uh, Mom? Can I ask you something?"

Oh, Lord, did he suspect something? Could he tell, even at sixteen, what she'd been up to? She looked around the room, but nothing screamed out, *Sex was had in this house today.* Still slightly wary, she returned her attention to her son. Had some of the kids done something to make him uncomfortable? Just because they lived in a rural area didn't mean there wasn't a possibility of drugs or underage drinking.

She braced herself. "Yes, dear. What is it?"

"You know how Kim's dad kind of disapproves of me, like, associating with her?"

Guilt sent a rush of heat to Emily's cheeks. Had someone seen her with Adam earlier and said something to David? Was he fishing for information?

Stop being paranoid or he will *get suspicious,* she scolded herself silently. "I think what Adam was objecting to the most was your giving her rides on your bike," she said. "When it comes to his daughter, he's a little overprotective."

David rolled his eyes. "Whatever. But what I wanted to know is whether *you* have any objections to me being around her." He began to tap one foot the way he often did when he was nervous. What was really going on here?

Emily shook her head. "As long as you respect her father's wishes," she said carefully, "and don't let her ride your bike or do anything else he might object to."

"Which is probably just about everything." David snorted. "Matt told me her dad's really strict with her, and I overheard Kim telling one of the other girls that he'd insisted on driving her to the last school dance. She sounded upset."

Emily couldn't fault his parenting. If she had a fifteen-year-old girl as pretty as Kim, she might have done the same thing. "Just be careful," she told David. "You know you can talk to me about anything."

He got to his feet, tipping back his head to finish his soda. "Thanks, Mom."

"Everything else okay?" she probed gently. "Did you get something to eat?"

He crushed the empty can with one hand, and she remembered the first time he'd done that as a child, pretending to be superstrong. "Yeah. We got burgers and fries. Are there any cookies?"

"In the jar on the counter," she replied. Fuel for the growing boy.

He stopped in the doorway and turned back to her. "Has Dad said anything to you about my visit?" he asked. "Do you know if he's bought my ticket yet?"

"I haven't talked to him." Emily debated

whether she should offer to call or have David do it. Dealing with her ex-husband was a pain, and having to exchange niceties with Stephanie if she happened to answer the phone was just as bad.

David shrugged. "He's probably just figuring out his schedule."

"I'll let you know if I hear from him," Emily said, taking the coward's way out. The last day of school was a month away, so there was no big rush. Besides, she wasn't looking forward to saying goodbye to her son, not even for a few weeks.

"Okay if I use the phone?" David asked. "I should call Kim's dad and see when he wants me to start my job."

Emily's first irrational impulse was to say no, just in case Adam should let something slip. Then common sense took over. What did she think, that he was going to *brag* about scoring with her to her own son? Her son who was looking at her oddly.

"Sure thing." She collected herself with an effort. "That's a good idea."

"The boy's a hard worker," said Charlie, Adam's youngest brother, as he removed his Broncos cap and mopped his brow with a navy-blue bandanna. "He's been bucking bales since the hay truck left."

Adam handed Charlie a jar of water from the cooler at their feet. He'd expected attitude or laziness or just plain incompetence from David, but he guessed he should have known better. The boy had his mother's genes, after all, and she had none of the above, except, perhaps, a little too much attitude.

"He's okay," Adam replied gruffly, watching David work. In the two weeks since Adam and Emily had started the affair they agreed had to be kept between the two of them for now, he never knew what to expect from her. The other day they had driven to a neighboring town for lunch after she'd shown him her studio, and they'd continued a lively discussion about books—rare, like the ones she'd shown him, and common.

Adam had enjoyed the lit class he'd taken in college, and he still loved to read when he had the time, but his taste had evolved to nonfiction, especially biographies from World War II. Emily had surprised him by admitting to a fondness for true crime and murder mysteries. He would have figured her for a reader of poetry or love stories, but when he'd suggested as much, she'd snorted rather inelegantly.

On his way home from dropping her off that day, he'd realized that, despite her limiting their physical contact to a few heated kisses, he'd enjoyed himself immensely. They'd argued, they'd laughed, and they had even agreed on a few minor points. He couldn't remember the last time he'd had such a good time with a woman out of bed.

A couple of days later she had called to reciprocate his lunch invitation, serving thick ham sandwiches and a chilled soup he'd found surprisingly good once they got around to eating it. She had met him at the door with a welcoming kiss that erupted between them like an explosion in a fireworks stand, resulting in a detour that left a trail of scattered clothing down the hallway to her bedroom and a frantic coupling Adam still got hard thinking about.

The memory of her slim, agile body wrapped around his, her silky skin and sweet taste, and her ability to strip every lucid thought from his mind made him squirm with discomfort while his sharp-eyed baby brother watched him curiously.

"Fleas?" Charlie asked, laughter dancing in his dark eyes. His twin dimples flashed when he grinned, as though he knew exactly where Adam's mind had been.

Adam snorted. "Not if your room's been fumigated."

"If I didn't have work to do, I'd take exception to that." Charlie set the empty jug next to the cooler.

"Wouldn't do you any good," Adam replied, more out of habit than a real wish to start anything.

Charlie scratched his chin, considering. "You're getting old, slowing down," he observed mildly. "Maybe it's time you stepped down, let a young dog start running things around here."

Adam moved back, putting a little more distance between them. He might have been willing to roll around in the dirt with his brother, just to prove he wasn't that old, but he didn't figure it would set a good example for the new hire. And Adam was wearing his good clothes.

"I've got a meeting in town, or I'd box your ears." The half truth rolled off his tongue. It was Emily he'd be meeting, and, technically, her place was on the way to Waterloo. Nice of Charlie to keep David busy for a couple more hours. Too bad Adam couldn't thank him for the favor.

Charlie looked him over. "You could always try, old man."

Maybe Adam would just clean up again later. Some things took priority, especially a brother who'd forgotten his place in the pecking order. Before he could decide, Charlie's gaze shifted to a spot beyond Adam's shoulder.

"She's growing up," he muttered.

Adam turned around to see Kim prancing toward them with an innocent expression that put him on full alert. She was wearing shorts that showed too much leg, a top that must have shrunk in the wash, and she'd done something to her eyes to make them look too damn sexy for a girl her age. In her hand was a plastic container in which Betty stored cookies.

"Hi, Daddy. Hi, Uncle Charlie." Her gaze slid in the direction of the hay shed, and her free hand went to her hair in a practiced movement Adam would have bet wasn't for his benefit or Charlie's. "I baked brownies, and I thought you might like some."

"I thought you were helping Rory today," Adam said.

"She and Travis took the kids to the movies," she replied, holding out the box. "I've got the afternoon off."

Charlie took a brownie and devoured it in two bites, his attention bouncing back and forth. "Mmm," he said, mouth full. "Really good, Kimmie. Why don't you offer a couple to the hired help. Take him some water, too."

"He's not due for a break yet," Adam growled, letting his annoyance show.

Charlie turned to glance at David, who was working with his back to them. "Hey, kid," he shouted. "Take five."

David's head snapped up, and Kim waved. "Thanks, Uncle Charlie," she purred, walking away before Adam could grab a brownie.

"What are you trying to promote?" he demanded when she was past hearing distance. "I ought to deck you, just on principle."

"It'd set a bad example." Charlie watched the two young people for a moment. "You raised her right. Now relax and let her spread her wings a little."

"She's too young," Adam argued. "I'm not such a doddering old man that I've forgotten what boys that age have on their minds and neither are you." He glared at his brother. "Hell, it's probably still all you think about."

Charlie turned to face him, his back to Kim and David. "Ease up, Dad. If you try to keep them apart, you'll only convince her he's the most interesting boy on the planet. I'll keep an eye on them."

"I can't tell you how reassuring that is."

Adam's voice dripped with sarcasm. "I can't wait till you have kids of your own."

"I can," Charlie said, dusting the rest of the brownie crumbs from his hands. "You've been even grumpier than usual lately. Maybe you need to go somewhere and get laid."

The abrupt change of subject caught Adam off guard. Something must have shown on his face, because Charlie narrowed his eyes.

"You've sure been gone a lot lately," he said thoughtfully. "Something you want to share with me, big brother? Have you found yourself a little playmate I don't know about?"

The implication that Emily was just some broad with round heels had Adam's hands curling into fists at his sides before he could stop himself. It was too much to hope that Charlie had missed the inadvertent gesture.

He stared down at Adam's fists with raised eyebrows.

"There's nothing going on," Adam blustered. "I'm too damn busy running this ranch to have time for anything else."

Once again Charlie shifted gears. "You doing okay?" he asked. "Cattle prices take another hit? Feed go up again?"

Adam shook his head. "No worse than usual."

"Things all right with Kimmie?" Charlie probed further.

Adam shrugged. He and both his brothers had always been tight. With their mother leaving and their old man always on one of them for screwing up somehow, they'd had to stick together.

"We're going through a rough patch," he confessed. "She argues about everything, and testing me has become her new hobby."

"I guess girls rebel, too," Charlie drawled. Hell, easy for him to say. "Remember some of the scrapes we got into. We're lucky we grew up alive."

"What do you think I'm worried about. If Kim ever tried any of the stuff we did, I'd nail her bedroom door shut with her inside."

"I still say you need to give her some room, bro," Charlie argued. "She'll make mistakes, sure, but she's a good kid."

"That's my point," Adam replied. "She's still a kid, and kids need rules. Talk to me again in a couple of years."

David had finished the water Kim had taken over to him as well as a couple of the brownies, glancing in Adam's direction several times. Good. Let the boy know that Adam was keeping an eye on him. He could hear his daughter's voice and her laughter, but not what she was saying. He was about to suggest that David get back to work when, with a final flip of her hair and a wave, Kim sauntered away.

Her chin was in the air and she was glaring when she approached Adam. "You were staring at us," she hissed. "Don't you trust me?"

Her snotty tone pissed him off. "Not when you strut around in front of the hired help like a working girl," he replied.

Her face went pale, and her blue eyes filled with tears. "I hate you!" she cried, flinging the plastic container at his feet and running over to where she'd left her bike.

"Well," Charlie said dryly as he bent to retrieve the abandoned box, "that went well." Opening it, he held it out to Adam. "Have a brownie."

Chapter Twelve

Emily was working late in the studio, gluing a special marbled paper to the inside cover of a family album she'd been commissioned to create. The design on the front of the goat-skin cover would be tooled in gold with the name of the family and the crest they'd had designed for them. New books comprised a small but lucrative part of Emily's business. People who wanted hand-bound family keepsakes had to be willing to pay the price.

She heard the screen door of the house slam, followed by David's feet pounding down the front steps. Did he ever move at a normal pace? Before she could insert the cover into one of the presses, the door to her studio flew open.

Emily swiveled around in her chair to remind him that startling her might result in disaster to a costly project. One look at his tear-streaked face, and she leaped to her feet, heart in her throat.

"What's happened? Are you all right?"

He never cried. Even when she'd told him they were moving, his response had been anger and shouted accusations, but the only tears shed that day were hers.

Quickly she set aside the half-forgotten cover and crossed the room, her gaze never leaving his flushed face. "Honey?" she asked again as she took his arm, "what's wrong? Is it Monty?" The dog was old; perhaps he'd collapsed.

"It's Dad!" David cried, pulling away from her. "How can he be so mean?"

Anger and alarm swirled together inside Emily as she circled around her son to peer into his face. If that man had done something to hurt him…

"Tell me." She struggled for calm. It wouldn't help David if she got upset, too.

"He says it's not convenient for me to visit right now." His tone was mimicking, mocking, underscored with pain. "He's too busy with work and their new baby."

Emily didn't know what to say. Deep down she'd been afraid of this all along. David had been counting on going, and Stuart was evasive. He'd taken his usual cowardly way out—not dealing with the situation until he absolutely had to, the same way he'd waited to confess his affair until Stephanie had gotten pregnant.

"He said that *maybe* I can come for Christmas," David choked out. "But he'll have to see."

"I'm sorry, honey." Emily reached out again, but he spun away.

"Christmas!" David wailed. "That's forever from now. My buddies will have forgotten that I exist by then."

Prudently Emily ignored the high drama and bit back the platitudes that crowded her tongue. He didn't want to hear that he could e-mail or write them, that real friends wouldn't forget him in a few months, that he was making a new life here. None of that would balance out the rejection by his father. When it came to his own flesh and blood, even a rat like Stuart could have been a little more sensitive.

"He's got his new family now, and he

doesn't need me anymore!" David glared at Emily. "It's all your fault!" His mouth twisted. "Why didn't you try to make him happy? We'd still be a family."

The unfairness of his attack struck her temporarily mute. Before she could find her voice, he turned and ran.

"I did try," Emily whispered past lips that trembled, but it was too late. He was gone.

For a moment her feet seemed rooted to the floor. Then she hurried outside as the thought struck her that he might roar off on his motorbike, too upset to drive sensibly. She saw him disappear instead into the stable.

Thank God for that! Chewing her lip indecisively, she wondered whether she should follow him. Try to reason with him. Part of her wanted to defend herself against his accusations, but she ignored the impulse. Perhaps a little time with the kittens that he often sat with and let climb all over him or the horses he never minded currying would calm him down. Meanwhile, Emily had a phone call to make.

With Adam's broodmares and their leggy foals in the private paddocks connected to each box stall, he'd been working in the barn for the past hour in the hopes that a little physical exercise might keep him from dwelling on Kim's angry words. A while ago he'd heard voices coming from outside, two of his men, but thankfully they'd walked on by.

Usually the mindless, repetitive chore of shoveling out stalls, the familiar smells of horse and leather and liniment, the relative silence and the steadying presence of his beloved Appaloosas enabled Adam to put things into perspective. In the year after Christie left, he'd spent a lot of time at the corral fence, staring unseeingly at the band of horses they'd kept for working cattle. Finding the strength to move on, praying for wisdom and guidance.

This time none of those things seemed to work. He could still hear his daughter's shrill voice as it cut through his heart like a scalpel.

I hate you.

He wouldn't have thought words could hurt so much. Sighing, he leaned on the shovel handle, absently rubbing his hand over a spot on his chest as though he could rub away the heartache they had caused.

He wondered what Kim was feeling right now. Rebellion? Remorse? She was stubborn, like him, which was why she needed a firm hand. She could be flighty and immature.

Were those faulty genes she'd gotten from her mother, or just a normal part of growing up?

How the hell was he supposed to guess?

Give him a calf or a foal and he knew what to do, but a teenager? His father's answer had been the belt or the back of his hand. Adam didn't believe in corporal punishment, even spanking. Maybe he was *too* lenient.

Dammit, how was he supposed to *know*? He thought of asking Travis, but his kids were little tykes. Rory was about to present him with another one. Charlie had made it clear he thought Adam was too strict.

He rotated the tightness from his shoulders, feeling a headache lurking. He'd called up to the house on his cell phone to let Betty know he wasn't coming in for dinner. Something in his voice must have warned her not to argue or else she'd talked to Kim, because instead of her usual fussing she had merely offered to leave him a plate.

The person Adam really wanted to confide in was Emily, but it was too early. They had agreed that ordinarily she would call him or else David might answer the phone at her end and get suspicious. Adam figured that his housekeeper had taken enough calls from Emily to know something was up, but she knew when to keep her thoughts to herself.

Adam tossed aside the shovel and lugged a saddle into the tack room. All this secrecy was getting annoying. Sooner or later, unless he and Emily stopped seeing each other, they would have to let their kids know that their parents had done exactly what the two of them had been forbidden to do—become involved.

He'd found that he was enjoying being involved, entangled and occasionally entwined with Ms. Major very much.

Before Adam could figure out how to convince her that it was time to bring their relationship into the open, the phone in the tack room rang, startling him. He'd installed it for emergencies, since most people called him on his cell.

"Yeah?" he answered warily. For a moment there was only silence. Shrugging, he was about to hang up.

"Adam?" asked a soft, familiar voice from his past. "Is that you?"

Ah, hell. Just what he needed to make his day complete.

"Hello, Christie," he replied grimly. "How's tricks?"

Emily slammed down the receiver before she could humiliate herself any further by bursting into tears of angry frustration. It had been bad enough to grit her teeth through Stephanie's attempts at polite chitchat while the baby fussed in the background, the new heir who had by all appearances usurped Emily's son's position in his father's heart. Still she'd forced herself to respond to the younger woman's questions as civilly as possible, unwilling to give the slightest impression that Stephanie's existence mattered to Emily one way or the other.

It had been Stuart's vague excuses, when he'd come on the line, and his total unwillingness to acknowledge the hurtful blow he'd dealt that had cranked her temper into the red zone.

Blast the man!

"David's a big boy," he'd said blithely. "He'll adjust. I'll send him a check. That should take his mind off his disappointment."

Smug bastard! Stuart still thought he could buy his way out of everything.

That was when Emily crashed the phone down in his ear. It had been either that or scream at him like the shrew he'd called her on more than one occasion since their split.

It was only after she'd hung up that angry tears had flooded her eyes and blurred her vision. Her hands shook. There was no way she'd get any more work done tonight.

Her eyes were still a little red and swollen, but she had managed to repair most of the damage. Sitting down on the leather couch, she studied the wildflower painting she'd picked up the other day, which Adam had helped her hang. After breathing deeply and counting to ten, she was headed outside to check on David when she saw a familiar pickup coming down the driveway. She recognized her son's friend, Matt, seated behind the wheel so she dredged up a smile of welcome and waited at the bottom of the steps while he pulled up and rolled down his window.

"Hi, Mrs. Major. Sorry I didn't call first, but I was just out riding around. Is Dave busy?"

She didn't want anyone catching her son with tear tracks drying on his face, but perhaps a visit from a contemporary would take his mind off his disappointment.

"I'll see if he's around," she offered. "Why don't you wait here?"

As soon as she'd cleared the way and Matt had joined David, she went back into the house, intent on calling Adam while she had a bit of privacy. Being a parent, surely he would lend a sympathetic ear.

Fifteen minutes later Emily pulled up outside the stable where Adam kept his horses. When she'd called his house, Mrs. Clark had mentioned that something had happened between Adam and Kim, and she had urged Emily to come. The idea that he might need her, that they could support each other, had been a tempting one, but now that she was here she was starting to have second thoughts.

What if Adam resented her interference? Although they'd talked a lot about their kids, talked about a variety of subjects when they weren't busy wearing each other out in bed, they certainly didn't always agree on how to raise them. Emily believed he was too strict with Kim, although she could understand why, and she suspected that he thought she'd been too lenient with David. On the other hand, Adam was the one who was pushing her to go public with their relationship, which she wasn't quite ready to do—especially after David's angry words this evening. If he felt as though his father had abandoned him, how would he deal with Emily getting involved with someone new?

And how would Kim react? From what Adam had said, she'd had him pretty much to herself until now. She was bound to feel some resentment.

Emily had to remind herself that none of these issues would matter if she and Adam didn't continue to see each other. Until now she had taken their relationship one day at a time, refusing to look past the here and now. What she hadn't counted on was her growing feelings for him. He made her feel sexy and feminine, alive and confident in ways she hadn't dreamed even existed. She'd been afraid to get involved with a man who might undermine her independence, but Adam respected it and her.

The scariest part was that she had no idea how he felt, or what he wanted from her. Before she could speculate any further, the man in her thoughts appeared in the open barn doorway. Backlit from inside, his size and shape made Emily's mouth go dry. If she hadn't had so much else on her mind, she would have been sorely tempted to tackle him into a haystack and see what developed.

While she was salivating, he turned so the light caught his face as he removed his baseball cap to wipe his forehead with his sleeve. He noticed her truck and his haggard expression was immediately replaced by a welcoming smile.

Feeling like a sneak, Emily glanced nervously around the deserted yard as she got out of her truck. She hadn't thought to make up an excuse for being here, in case anyone asked. She'd been in too much of a hurry to see Adam.

"Hi," she said, some of her anxiety melting away at the warmth in his eyes. "I hope it's okay that I just came by. I—"

Adam interrupted her babble by grabbing her shoulders and planting a kiss on her mouth. Emily sagged against him, hungrily parting her lips so that he would deepen the kiss. Adam complied with her silent request, but too soon he pulled away, resting his forehead against hers.

"Do you have some kind of feminine radar?" he asked as he straightened and grabbed her hand. "How did you know how desperately I needed to see you?"

"Betty told me."

He glanced over his shoulder as he led her into the barn. "She called you?"

"No, I was calling you. She told me you were down here." She ran her hands over his chest, savoring his strength, trying to soak some of it up as the events of her evening came flooding back. "Why did you need me?" she asked curiously. Had it just been a figure of speech?

He rolled his eyes. "First, I had a nasty scene with Princess Kimmie, and then Christie called a little while ago."

"Your ex-wife? I didn't know you two kept in touch." Emily experienced a surge of jealousy that was probably out of line. She had no right to feel possessive, not this early on, but somehow the green-eyed monster didn't care about timing.

Adam led her to a padded leather bench and sat down with his arm draped over her shoulders. "She's written to Kim a few times and recently she's called her, but—no big surprise—Kim's been less than receptive." His face was in profile, his jaw set. He didn't look pleased.

"She's still hurt," Emily commented, thinking of David. "After what you've told me about the way her mother ignored her for so long, who could blame Kim for feeling the way she does?"

"Yeah," he replied, fatigue in his voice, "Christie's got a lot to make up for."

"Is that why she called?" Emily asked, rubbing his forearm in an effort to convey her support.

"She wants me to intercede for her, but I

haven't decided yet what to do." He turned his head, his gaze meeting Emily's as a frown pleated his forehead. "What do you think?"

Emily recalled Stuart's indifference. "Do you think she's serious?"

"Who knows. We talked for several minutes, and she seems to be. I tried to make her understand how much damage she'd cause if she does come back into Kim's life and then goes away again." He laced his fingers through Emily's. "Part of me wants to tell her to forget it, but Kim's growing up. I'm her father, and I love her, but I'm a guy. You know what I'm saying?" He looked helpless, his grin crooked.

"I have a teenage son," Emily reminded him dryly, recalling a few awkward conversations she'd had with David. "Believe me, I know."

"So what do you think I should do?" Adam asked.

"Maybe you should give her a chance," Emily replied. "If it works out, it will be wonderful for Kim. If not, you'll be here to pick up the pieces."

Adam gazed down at her with approval in his gaze. "How did you get to be so wise?" he asked softly.

"You won't think so when I tell you about

my evening," she retorted. While he listened, she filled him in on what David had told her and her subsequent conversation with his father. By the time she was finished, she was trembling with renewed frustration.

"Too many ex-spouses in our evening," he said lightly. "Your son blames you for your divorce and my daughter hates me." He got to his feet, pulling Emily up with him.

"Oh, no," she exclaimed, "I'm sure she didn't mean that, any more than David believes what he told me—not deep down, anyway."

Adam rested his palm against her cheek. "You're right. Thank you."

"Right back at you." She returned his smile.

"I know just the thing to make us both feel better." With a rakish grin, he dipped his head. Emily met him halfway, and it was several long moments before they came up for air. When they did, his breathing had quickened and his expression was serious. "I know it's too soon to say this, but I have to give you fair warning," he said, voice rough. "I'm falling for you, Emily, and it's scary as hell."

Before she could reply, a slim feminine figure walked into the glow from the overhead light, hands parked on her hips. "Oh, isn't this just too, too cozy!" Kim sneered with a toss of her long, dark hair. "You two make me want to barf."

Chapter Thirteen

For a moment the three of them stood frozen in the artificial light. Emily's cheeks flamed with embarrassment that she'd been seen kissing Adam with such total abandon.

"Kim," she said in an instinctive effort to smooth over the awkward moment, but then she faltered, having no idea what to say to the girl who was clearly so upset.

"I knew you were after him," Kim cried, pointing an accusing finger at Emily. "I could tell by the way you were practically drooling when we saw you in town."

Emily realized the poor girl felt threatened by her interest in the only parent Kim really knew. Before Emily could figure out what to say, Adam shifted so that he was standing in front of her like a shield. The gesture wasn't lost on Kim, who turned pale.

"Young lady, you have no right to be so rude," he said angrily. "Go on back to the house right this minute. I'll talk to you later."

Kim flinched as though he'd hit her. "So you can finish what the two of you started?" she lashed out. "Rolling around and groping each other in the hay!"

"Kim!" His voice snapped like a whip. "You heard me!"

Emily wished there was something, anything, she could say to defuse the situation. Of course, Kim shouldn't be acting this way, but it was plain to see how upset she was, and Adam's heavy-handed parenting wasn't helping. As Kim continued to stare at them defiantly, her body shaking with emotion, Emily put her hand on his arm.

Impatiently he pulled away, embarrassing her further in front of his daughter.

"I'll take care of this," he said gruffly.

Clearly he didn't need or want Emily's input. "Why don't I just wait in my pickup," she said quietly.

Before she could leave, he snaked his arm around her shoulders and pulled her close. "Kim," he said, "I told you to go back to the house. Now do what I told you." It was obvious he was used to having his orders obeyed.

He was treating Kim like a child, but Emily wasn't sure just how *she* would react if David had been the one to catch them in such a compromising position. This was exactly why she'd been reluctant to see him openly. Perhaps if she could have gotten to know Kim a little better, the girl wouldn't be so upset now or feel so threatened.

Kim glared at her with pure malice. "Sorry I interrupted your make-out session." She spun away on a sob and ran out of the stable.

Adam let out a long sigh and removed his arm from Emily's shoulders. "At least this time she didn't tell me she hates me."

Emily could see the frustration in his face. "Maybe you'd better go after her," she suggested gently. "I'll go home, and you can call me later. I need to talk to David before someone else does."

Adam tucked a strand of hair behind her ear, his gaze searching hers. "What a mess," he murmured. "She has no right to talk that way."

"She's upset," Emily responded. "And she's worried about losing you."

He snorted at the idea, and then he rubbed the back of his neck with one hand. "Damn," he muttered. "All this made me forget about Christie's phone call." He flexed his shoulders as though they were holding up the weight of the world. "I hate to let you leave, but I suppose you're right. Go talk to your boy, and I'll deal with Kim."

Emily was dismayed at his grim tone. Did he understand what his daughter must be feeling? If he handled things badly, she'd resent Emily more than she did already. Like he'd said, what a mess.

"Maybe we should stop seeing each other," Emily suggested softly.

He took a step back, hands on his hips. A muscle jumped in his cheek as he studied her. "Is that what you want?"

To stop herself from throwing her arms around his neck, She threaded the fingers of both hands together in front of her. "No, not really, but it might be best for all concerned."

Frowning darkly, Adam hauled her into his arms. "I don't believe that," he whispered into her hair as he held her tight against him. "And I'm not ready to give you up."

After Emily had driven away, Adam watched the taillights of her silly little pickup until they disappeared around the curve past Travis's house. Then he braced his hands against the small of his back and stretched the knots from his spine.

God, what a day! He was in no hurry to deal with his daughter. Too damn much had happened. And Emily hadn't even reacted to his declaration. Had she even heard him when he'd admitted he was falling for her?

He reminded himself that she, too, had a lot on her plate right now. Damn, but her ex was a jerk! Adam could hardly blame her if she was reluctant to get serious again.

Or maybe she didn't feel the same way he did. Until they could talk again, he refused to speculate.

After he'd shut the door to the stable, he began walking down the road toward his house. The cool air felt good against his hot face. As always, being surrounded by Winchester land made him feel as though he had done something right in his life. Too bad the old man hadn't lasted long enough to see what the ranch would become. What his son had made of it.

Before Adam confronted Kim, he needed to figure out what the hell he was going to say. How much had she seen before she barged in on them? Had she heard what he'd said to Emily? He felt a little like a teenager who'd been caught groping his girl in the back seat of his Chevy.

And Kim wondered why he was in no hurry for her to grow up and start dating!

Maybe Emily was right. Maybe he'd been naive to think his daughter would welcome a new woman into their lives. He'd figured his only problem would be making her understand why he still didn't want her getting involved with David.

Ha! If only life were that simple!

All the emotion of the past few hours, the scenes with Kim, Christie's call, plus his growing love for his feisty neighbor—something he'd never expected—were all churning together in his gut like a lumpy batch of concrete in a mixer truck. As he walked, he rubbed absently at his stomach, realizing that he hadn't eaten since lunch. It was getting late, and Kim had school in the morning. Maybe it would be better if he waited until tomorrow to talk to her, after they'd both had time to calm down.

Emily spent the morning cooking up a storm, something she liked to do when she had a lot on her mind. Spending time in the kitchen gave her time to think, and she'd also been meaning to take Rory a casserole.

They'd talked on the phone a few times, and Emily had sent her a card after one minor scare sent her to the doctor, but Adam had taken up a lot of Emily's time, as had her work. She was dying to know what had happened with Kim, but he hadn't called.

Now, because Emily was so distracted, she did some heavy-duty baking as well as fixing a pan of lasagna and a double batch of spaghetti sauce. She added a container of sauce to the box for Rory, as well as a pan of brownies, the casserole and an apple pie.

After Rory thanked her, eyes sparkling with pleasure, the two women settled on the wide front porch with tall glasses of iced tea and a plate of peanut butter cookies that Adam's housekeeper had brought down the day before.

Before Emily quite knew what was happening, she'd succumbed to her new friend's willingness to listen. Emily didn't feel it was her place to tell Rory about Kim's outburst or to mention Adam's call from his ex-wife. Instead she described Stuart's latest unfeeling stunt.

"The bastard!" Rory exclaimed when she was through unloading. "I'll bet you're glad to be free of him." She was sitting with her hand resting on her rounded stomach and her feet propped up because her ankles were swollen. Her glorious red hair was anchored to the top of her head with a huge plastic claw imbedded with silver glitter. She'd told Emily it had been a gift from her children. With only a couple weeks till her due date, she'd admitted to being more than ready to meet her baby and put this whole episode behind her.

"The next time Travis comes at me with that gleam in his eye, I'm liable to grab the nearest bat and start swinging," she'd told Emily with a throaty laugh.

Emily hadn't looked at her latest confrontation with Stuart from the angle of being free of him. Trust Rory to put a positive spin on it.

"Yes, you're right," she admitted after she'd taken a sip of iced tea. "It was a wake-up call to remind me how self-centered Stuart always was." A few of the knots in her stomach loosened. "I don't envy his new wife." With a start, she realized the words were true. She *didn't* envy Stephanie—hadn't since the move to Colorado.

"In time she'll find out that Stuart is all about things and possessions," she continued, feeling lighter. "But they don't take the place of being married to someone who's a real partner, like Travis is to you." He'd taken both children for the day, just to give Rory a rest. What a gem!

"So are you seeing anyone?" Rory asked casually as she helped herself to a cookie. "Despite what you told me before, you do have that certain glow about you that women just can't hide from other, more envious women."

"What glow is that?" Emily could feel a flush warming her cheeks. Could Rory really tell, or was she just fishing? Maybe Adam had said something to Travis, kind of a one-man-to-another thing.

"The glow of a woman who's not sleeping alone," Rory said, sounding disgruntled. "The glow I won't have again until I get the doctor's okay."

"Did Adam say something about me?" Emily blurted.

Rory's mouth curved into a wide grin. "Bingo!" She clapped her hands together in obvious glee. "I was right. Travis owes me a shopping trip to Denver after I get my figure back."

Emily realized she'd been duped. "How *did* you know?"

"Adam hasn't said one word about buying your land in weeks," Rory replied, "and he's been smiling a lot lately, which is *very* unusual for Adam, believe me. Add the way you two managed to avoid eye contact the entire time we talked to you after church last week, and I figured something had to be up."

"That's pretty thin," Emily protested. Was he smiling more because he thought he'd figured out another way to get her land?

"It's not thin when you know Travis's elder brother." Rory heaved herself out of her chair. "I'll be right back. I have to pee."

Emily wasn't overly concerned when David didn't show up right after school, but by dinnertime she was beginning to worry because he hadn't even called. Had she mixed up his work schedule at the ranch? Finally, when the lasagna she'd fixed was ready to serve and he still wasn't home, she turned down the oven temperature and called Adam's cell phone.

What he told her left Emily shaken, her dinner forgotten.

Kim was missing, too. One of her friends had finally admitted that Kim was talking about running away.

As soon as Emily told him about David, he'd leaped to the conclusion that this was all her son's fault. Before Adam had hung up to alert the sheriff's office, despite her pleas that he hold off for a little while longer, he'd demanded the license number and description of David's motorbike.

Numbly Emily turned off the oven and put the salad she'd made into the fridge, her appetite gone. Adam had said that one of the younger ranch hands told him Kim and David had been spending a lot of time together while David was working. Kim's girlfriend admitted that Kim and David hung out together at school.

Would David have been upset enough to do something as foolish as running off with her, the way Adam suspected, or was he somewhere else entirely? He'd been pretty quiet this morning before school, but Emily had assumed he was still struggling with his disappointment over the canceled trip.

Glancing at the phone every few minutes in the hopes that he would contact her before Adam called out the militia, Emily flipped restlessly through a decorating magazine. She couldn't focus enough to risk working on any of her valuable projects. Even Wes's painting failed to soothe her. Finally she gave up and was about to turn on the television when the phone rang shrilly, making her drop the remote.

Mumbling a quick prayer, she picked up the receiver with a hand that trembled.

"Mom?"

Sagging with relief, Emily sank into a chair. "Where are you?"

"I'm with Kim. We're at the bus station in Elizabeth, but she doesn't want to call her dad." He sounded worn-out. "Could you bring the truck for my bike and pick us up?"

Her hand tightened on the phone. "What's going on? I've been worried sick and so has Adam."

"Can we talk about it later?" he pleaded.

If the two of them had planned to leave together and then something had changed their minds, she wasn't about to ply him with questions now.

"Of course," she replied, thinking fast, "but I will have to call Kim's father and let him know she's all right."

He must have put his hand over the receiver, but she could hear muffled voices. Finally he came back on the line. "Okay," he said, "but don't bring him with you, okay? Just come by yourself."

"I'll do my best, but I can't promise that." Emily's mind raced. "Give me your word that you'll wait for me, that you won't take off before I get there."

There was a long pause, during which she held her breath. Were they old enough to buy bus tickets on their own? She had no idea. Or what if they caught a ride with some creep? The idea of that made her shudder.

"We'll be here, but don't take too long, okay? Kim's still pretty upset."

"I'll leave as soon as I call Adam." When David broke the connection, she immediately redialed. Adam would probably be irate, but he would have to agree the important thing was that the kids were okay.

He answered his cell on the first ring.

"David just called," she said excitedly. "They're both all right."

She wasn't entirely prepared for his angry reaction. "So my first instincts were correct," he burst out. "I should never have let that delinquent within a hundred miles of my daughter."

Emily was tempted to slam down the phone, but she resisted. "I don't have time to debate that with you now," she said through clenched teeth. "I'm going to pick them up, and I'll bring Kim straight home."

"Wait a minute! I'm going with you. Where are they?"

"She wants me to come alone."

"The hell with that!" he exclaimed. "I'm leaving for your place right now."

Emily chewed on her lip, trying to decide how to change his mind.

"She's underage," he reminded her. "Either you tell me where they are, or I'll call the sheriff again."

Adam had been able to tell when he got to her place that she was unhappy about his coming along, but there was no way he could sit at home twiddling his thumbs. Besides, neither of their trucks would seat four people safely.

At least she hadn't left without him, but when he got there, she'd driven past his truck with her window rolled up, barely glancing at him. He'd had to honk his horn and cut her off before she would tell him where they were headed.

The bus station! He still wasn't clear why Kim hadn't called him. Perhaps David, fearful of reprisals, wouldn't let her.

As soon as Adam turned onto the main road, he pulled out around Emily's truck and floored the accelerator. Her surprised face flashed by as he barreled past her. If her son had done anything to hurt Kim, Adam's relationship with Emily might be damaged beyond repair, but he'd have to put his own selfish needs on hold until he found out what the hell had been going on with his daughter.

When he pulled up in front of the building that housed the small bus station, with Emily practically riding his bumper, he immediately recognized the two runaways waiting out front. David's scooter was parked at the curb. His helmet and Kim's school bag were on the sidewalk next to her feet. Her head jerked around, and then she said something to David. They appeared to argue, and he grabbed her arm.

The sight of the boy touching Kim sent fresh rage roaring through Adam as he got out of his truck.

"Adam!" Emily called out from behind him.

He didn't even hesitate as he heard her door slam. Instead he hurried over to where Kim was standing with her arms folded across her chest and her head bent. His relief at seeing her in one piece was blotted out by his anger at her refusal to acknowledge him.

"Come on," he told her as Emily caught up with him. "Let's go."

Emily reached out to squeeze David's arm. "You okay?" she asked softly. He responded with a jerky nod. Sunglasses hid Emily's eyes, and her cheeks were pale. She was clearly upset. Adam felt a pang of regret for the wedge this mess had driven between them.

"Why did you bring *him?*" Kim asked Emily.

Adam had no intention of hashing this out on the sidewalk. "I came to bring you home."

"Take it easy on her, okay?" David chimed in. "She's been kind of upset."

Only the boy's youth kept Adam from decking him right there. "I suppose this was all your idea," he sneered instead. "Just where were you taking her?"

David returned his glare without flinching, but neither did he answer.

"I asked you a question." Adam's blood pressure climbed another notch.

Unexpectedly Kim grabbed his arm. "Can we just go? I'll tell you what happened on the way home." She sent a beseeching glance at David that strained Adam's control even further. "Please, Daddy?" she repeated. "It's not his fault."

"Come on, son. Let's go home," Emily suggested. "Let them sort this out between them."

Adam shook his finger at the boy. "I'm not done with you."

"Daddy!" Kim exclaimed again as two

young kids rode by on scooters. An old lady with two shopping bags walked past them going the other way.

"Okay, okay." Adam glanced at the motorbike. "Do you need help getting that loaded?" He didn't want Emily hurt.

"I can manage, thanks," David replied politely.

Emily didn't say anything, so Adam opened the driver's door and looked at her over the top of it. "I'll talk to you," he said.

She gave him what could only be described as a *look,* but she didn't reply. Suddenly all the fight went out of Adam, replaced by a wave of exhaustion. Fastening his seat belt, he started the engine and prepared to deal with his daughter.

"Let's stop and get something to eat," Emily suggested to David as they drove past a little pizza joint. She had no appetite, but her insides felt shaky. A large part of her heart was breaking, but she had too many other issues to deal with before she could give in to the pain and disappointment weighing her down. "You can tell me what's going on."

David was slouched next to her. He hadn't said a word since they loaded his motorbike into the bed of the truck. "Okay."

Emily waited until they'd been seated in a booth and their order taken by a gum-popping young waitress who'd given David the once-over before she ambled away.

"Well?" Emily asked after she'd taken a sip of her water. What she probably needed was a drink!

"This wasn't my idea, Mom, I swear," David began.

Relief flooded through her, followed immediately by concern for both Adam and his daughter. He'd been so angry, so quick to blame *her* son. His attitude had been a real eye opener, and the poor girl looked so miserable.

"What happened?" Emily asked quietly.

"First off, Kim's not my girlfriend," David said. "Not that I wouldn't be interested, but she's too mixed up right now."

"Go on," Emily prompted him.

"We've gotten to be friends, though, and we talk a lot, you know? Her dad's so strict. He doesn't ever really listen, and she's all confused about her mom." He leaned forward, fiddling with a container of grated cheese. "Today at school Kim told me she was going to take off. She had money in her backpack and everything. I tried to talk her out of it, but she said she was going to catch a ride to

Denver, to find where her mom lives. I didn't know what to do."

"You could have called me," Emily suggested dryly.

He gave her a look of disbelief. "Anyway, I talked her into taking the bus instead, to stall, you know? And then I gave her a ride to Elizabeth. I was afraid she'd bolt if she saw me using the phone. Finally she agreed to let me call." He shrugged. "You know the rest. I don't suppose Adam will let me keep working for him now. I kind of liked that job."

Emily reached across the table and put her hand on his. "You did the right thing. You kept Kim safe, and maybe Adam will figure that out."

It had been two weeks to the day since Adam had picked Kim up in Elizabeth, two weeks since he'd seen Emily. After Kim admitted the truth about her attempt to run away, he'd called David to apologize and make sure the boy knew he had a job at the ranch if he still wanted it.

So much had happened. Adam and Kim had talked, really talked. He'd assured her she would always be important to him, but he'd also admitted his feelings for Emily. Kim had talked to Christie a couple of times, and they'd been e-mailing each other. He'd agreed that Kim could visit her mother this summer. Best of all, Rory had given birth to a healthy baby boy just a few days ago. Adam had been at the hospital to see Travis's happy tears and to tease him about Rory's threats, overheard out in the family lounge while she was in hard labor.

Now Adam was on his way over to Travis's house to fix a damn broken pipe. Travis had claimed he didn't have time, with three kids and a recuperating wife to deal with. When Adam pulled up with his toolbox, he nearly backed around and left again. Emily's truck was parked behind the house.

Before he could make up his mind, Travis came out onto the porch. "Never knew you for a coward, big bro," he said with an infuriating grin.

Adam swore under his breath and got out of the truck. "I smell a setup," he growled, lugging the toolbox he probably didn't even need.

Travis clapped him on the back. "Blame it on the kids," he said as he led the way inside. A crying baby could be heard from upstairs.

Adam stopped dead in his tracks. "What kids? What do you mean?"

"Kim and David have been plotting to get

you two back together," Travis replied, glancing at the top of the stairs. "Guess it worked."

Adam's heart began to thud harder when he recognized Emily coming down toward them. As soon as she spotted him, she hesitated, her hand tightening on the banister. Then she resumed her descent, cheeks flushed.

"Travis, the baby's a doll and that's quite a shock of red hair. You must be very proud." She didn't even glance at Adam.

Travis looked awfully damn smug. If this backfired, Adam was going to drown him in the stock tank. "Yes, ma'am," Travis replied with a big wink at Adam. "Guess I'll go up right now and take another *long* look at the little critter. You two take your time, get caught up on the gossip around town. You won't be interrupted. I'm going to visit with my wife, and Kim's watching my other two monsters down by the orchard. They took a picnic lunch."

Silently both Adam and Emily watched him leave as though they'd never seen anyone climb stairs before. Then Emily looked at Adam for the first time.

"I didn't know you'd be here." Her tone implied that if she had she'd be miles away.

Adam planted his hand over his pounding heart. "I swear I had no part in this."

She shrugged, eyes chilly. "No matter. How's Kim doing?"

Despite his inner turmoil, he couldn't keep a smile from forming. "She's fine, going to visit her mother next month."

Emily didn't appear surprised. "That's what David told me. Thank you for not firing him. He enjoys the work a lot."

"I had no reason to let him go," Adam admitted. "He's a good worker, and he's getting to be a better rider all the time."

She acknowledged his comment with a nod. "He's saving his wages for a car."

"I know. We've been discussing the different models."

Clearly the comment surprised her. "You and *David?*"

"Yeah. He's a good kid. You've done a great job. I offered to help him look at cars when the time comes." He couldn't read her reaction at all. "If it's okay with you," he added hastily.

From upstairs they could hear the faint sound of people's voices, a high-pitched giggle followed by a door shutting and then silence. How Adam envied his brother what he had found with Rory.

Emily nibbled at her lower lip, sending a surge of longing through him. Damn, but he'd missed her. He just hadn't known what to say to make up for acting like such a jerk, for jumping to conclusions.

"That would be okay, I guess," she said finally. "If it's what he wants to do and you have the time." She glanced at her watch. "Well, I'd better be going. Nice seeing you." She attempted to duck around him, but he blocked her way.

Her gaze flew to his.

"David's forgiven me," Adam blurted. "Can't you?"

To his dismay, tears filled her eyes as she continued to gaze up at him. Unable to stop himself, he swept her into his arms and buried his face in her hair. "I've missed you," he murmured.

"I've missed you, too." Her voice was small, sad. He held her away from him so he could see her face.

"What is it?" he asked, but she only shook her head.

He took a deep breath and dived in. "I told you something the last time we were alone, but you never responded," he reminded her.

She relieved him by blinking away her tears before they could fall. Women's tears panicked him. "And what was that?" she asked.

Adam swallowed hard. "I told you I was falling for you."

"I remember." Her expression softened slightly. "We were interrupted."

"Yes. Well, what I told you about my feelings isn't exactly true anymore."

His words were like ice to Emily. Ever since she'd first seen him standing there in Rory's house, her heart had been flip-flopping nervously in the hopes he'd somehow come by to see her. Then when he'd talked about David, the tiny spark of hope had grown. But now he was telling her his feelings had changed.

"I'm sorry to hear that," she said evenly, praying for a chance to escape before she totally broke down. As long as she hadn't actually seen him, she could still believe they might work out their differences. Now she had to acknowledge that she'd been living in fantasyland.

To her surprise Adam reached for her hands. "I realize I've made some bad mistakes that hurt you," he said, "but I have to tell you the most important thing I've learned in the past couple of weeks."

"What's that?" she asked through lips that had grown numb.

"That I'm done falling. I'm all the way in love with you. Is there any hope at all that you could forgive me for being such a dolt? Give me a chance to make it up to you?" Tenderness and something else—uncertainty, perhaps—shone in his eyes.

For a moment his words made no sense to her.

His fingers tightened on hers. "Emily?"

Had he really said he loved her? Happiness burst inside her as her bemused brain started functioning again. "I don't need time!" she cried.

His hopeful expression faded, so she grasped the lapels on his leather vest and rose up on her tiptoes. "I've fallen, too," she whispered. "All the way."

Adam tipped his head as he caught her in his arms. His lips covered hers in a kiss that was both joyful and satisfyingly passionate. When he finally lifted his head, Emily's knees were trembling and fresh tears had blurred her vision.

"In that case, there's one more thing I have to say." His voice was shaking. "I know it hasn't been very long, but when something's right, there's no calendar. I want you to spend your life with me."

When she didn't answer, he gave her a squeeze and let her go. "I'm sorry. I didn't mean to rush you."

"No, it's not that." Happiness bubbled inside her. "The only problem is with my land. Mr. Johnson made me promise I'd never sell it to a Winchester. Do you know why he felt that way?"

Adam looked totally confused. "No. We wondered why he hadn't just come to us first, instead of being so secretive. He didn't give you a reason?"

"He didn't say, so I didn't ask."

He rubbed the back of his neck thoughtfully. "Hmm. So what exactly does that mean?"

"Well," Emily mused, resting one hand lightly along the side of his face, savoring his warmth and letting herself finally accept that she'd found the happiness she hadn't even realized she'd been looking for when she'd come here, "I promised him I'd never let the land fall into my awful neighbor's hands, but I never said I wouldn't share it with my husband."

* * * * *

WESTERN WP PROMISES

YES! Please send me **The Western Promises Collection** in Larger Print. This collection begins with 3 FREE books and 2 FREE gifts (gifts valued at approx. $14.00 retail) in the first shipment, along with the other first 4 books from the collection! If I do not cancel, I will receive 8 monthly shipments until I have the entire 51-book Western Promises collection. I will receive 2 or 3 FREE books in each shipment and I will pay just $4.99 US/ $5.89 CDN for each of the other four books in each shipment, plus $2.99 for shipping and handling per shipment. *If I decide to keep the entire collection, I'll have paid for only 32 books, because 19 books are FREE! I understand that accepting the 3 free books and gifts places me under no obligation to buy anything. I can always return a shipment and cancel at any time. My free books and gifts are mine to keep no matter what I decide.

272 HCN 3070 472 HCN 3070

Name	(PLEASE PRINT)	
Address		Apt. #
City	State/Prov.	Zip/Postal Code

Signature (if under 18, a parent or guardian must sign)

Mail to the **Reader Service**:

IN U.S.A.: P.O. Box 1867, Buffalo, NY 14240-1867
IN CANADA: P.O. Box 609, Fort Erie, Ontario L2A 5X3

WPBPA16R

REQUEST YOUR FREE BOOKS!
2 FREE NOVELS PLUS 2 FREE GIFTS!

HARLEQUIN®

SPECIAL EDITION

Life, Love & Family

YES! Please send me 2 FREE Harlequin® Special Edition novels and my 2 FREE gifts (gifts are worth about $10). After receiving them, if I don't wish to receive any more books, I can return the shipping statement marked "cancel." If I don't cancel, I will receive 6 brand-new novels every month and be billed just $4.74 per book in the U.S. or $5.49 per book in Canada. That's a savings of at least 12% off the cover price! It's quite a bargain! Shipping and handling is just 50¢ per book in the U.S. and 75¢ per book in Canada.* I understand that accepting the 2 free books and gifts places me under no obligation to buy anything. I can always return a shipment and cancel at any time. Even if I never buy another book, the two free books and gifts are mine to keep forever.

235/335 HDN GH3Z

Name _____ (PLEASE PRINT) _____

Address _____ Apt. # _____

City _____ State/Prov. _____ Zip/Postal Code _____

Signature (if under 18, a parent or guardian must sign)

Mail to the **Reader Service**:
IN U.S.A.: P.O. Box 1867, Buffalo, NY 14240-1867
IN CANADA: P.O. Box 609, Fort Erie, Ontario L2A 5X3

Want to try two free books from another line?
Call 1-800-873-8635 or visit www.ReaderService.com.

* Terms and prices subject to change without notice. Prices do not include applicable taxes. Sales tax applicable in N.Y. Canadian residents will be charged applicable taxes. Offer not valid in Quebec. This offer is limited to one order per household. Not valid for current subscribers to Harlequin Special Edition books. All orders subject to credit approval. Credit or debit balances in a customer's account(s) may be offset by any other outstanding balance owed by or to the customer. Please allow 4 to 6 weeks for delivery. Offer available while quantities last.

Your Privacy—The Reader Service is committed to protecting your privacy. Our Privacy Policy is available online at www.ReaderService.com or upon request from the Reader Service.

We make a portion of our mailing list available to reputable third parties that offer products we believe may interest you. If you prefer that we not exchange your name with third parties, or if you wish to clarify or modify your communication preferences, please visit us at www.ReaderService.com/consumerchoice or write to us at Reader Service Preference Service, P.O. Box 9062, Buffalo, NY 14240-9062. Include your complete name and address.

HSE15

REQUEST YOUR FREE BOOKS!
2 FREE NOVELS PLUS 2 FREE GIFTS!

HARLEQUIN®

American Romance®

LOVE, HOME & HAPPINESS

YES! Please send me 2 FREE Harlequin® American Romance® novels and my 2 FREE gifts (gifts are worth about $10). After receiving them, if I don't wish to receive any more books, I can return the shipping statement marked "cancel." If I don't cancel, I will receive 4 brand-new novels every month and be billed just $4.74 per book in the U.S. or $5.49 per book in Canada. That's a savings of at least 12% off the cover price! It's quite a bargain! Shipping and handling is just 50¢ per book in the U.S. and 75¢ per book in Canada.* I understand that accepting the 2 free books and gifts places me under no obligation to buy anything. I can always return a shipment and cancel at any time. Even if I never buy another book, the two free books and gifts are mine to keep forever.

154/354 HDN GHZZ

Name	(PLEASE PRINT)	
Address		Apt. #
City	State/Prov.	Zip/Postal Code

Signature (if under 18, a parent or guardian must sign)

Mail to the **Reader Service:**
IN U.S.A.: P.O. Box 1867, Buffalo, NY 14240-1867
IN CANADA: P.O. Box 609, Fort Erie, Ontario L2A 5X3

Want to try two free books from another line?
Call 1-800-873-8635 or visit www.ReaderService.com.

* Terms and prices subject to change without notice. Prices do not include applicable taxes. Sales tax applicable in N.Y. Canadian residents will be charged applicable taxes. Offer not valid in Quebec. This offer is limited to one order per household. Not valid for current subscribers to Harlequin American Romance books. All orders subject to credit approval. Credit or debit balances in a customer's account(s) may be offset by any other outstanding balance owed by or to the customer. Please allow 4 to 6 weeks for delivery. Offer available while quantities last.

Your Privacy—The Reader Service is committed to protecting your privacy. Our Privacy Policy is available online at www.ReaderService.com or upon request from the Reader Service.

We make a portion of our mailing list available to reputable third parties that offer products we believe may interest you. If you prefer that we not exchange your name with third parties, or if you wish to clarify or modify your communication preferences, please visit us at www.ReaderService.com/consumerschoice or write to us at Reader Service Preference Service, P.O. Box 9062, Buffalo, NY 14240-9062. Include your complete name and address.

HAR15